# Taboo

# Ann Jennings

Maximize Publishing Inc.

P.O. Box 930665

Norcross Ga 30093

Attn.: Michael McCain

C/o: Kevin Brown

Kelby Lott

Maximize Publishing Inc.
ISBN-13: 978-0692405215
ISBN-10: 0692405216

Ann Jennings
TABOO

# Taboo

# Ann Jennings

Ann Jennings
TABOO

"He doesn't love you", Charlotte was saying to her cousin and best friend Amanda Marie Collins for the tenth time in thirty minutes while they talked on the phone. Just because you and Gunnar have two beautiful children together doesn't mean he loves you Charlotte preached. After sixteen years he should have married you and made you his wife. I wish I wouldn't have taken you out with me sixteen years ago that night and you would never have met Mr. Gunnar D. Bradley Charlotte preached.

At least He's raising his kids and he's a good father Amanda cried. I didn't say he wasn't a good father Charlotte declared. I'm just saying you love him more than he loves you. But I do so much for him Amanda declared why doesn't he love me? Charlotte breathed heavy into the phone and sided, maybe you do too much for him.  He didn't marry Traci his ex-girlfriend and they have two kids together Charlotte offered.

Yes I know Amanda cried I was hoping this time would be different. Gunnar will never change Charlotte quoted he will always be Gunnar. He gives me everything I want Amanda offered everything but the one thing you want most Charlotte preached, love. He loves me Amanda mumbled just in his own way and then she started to cry into the phone. Please don't do that again Charlotte demanded you know I hate it when you cry. I don't know what else to do Amanda pronounced. Go to church with me tomorrow then we'll go to Red Lobster and talk Charlotte said. Ok Amanda sighed I'll see you tomorrow. When Amanda hung up the phone from her cousin she laid back on her pillow and cried for two and a half hours. After crying Amanda got up and sat in her window seat in her bedroom to do some serious thinking about her future.

It was a cold November day in Michigan the snow was falling and everything outside was covered in white. Her parents Jonnie and Frank still lived in New York and they were experiencing heavy snow also, when Amanda talked to her mom yesterday she said it had been snowing for three days straight. Amanda didn't regret moving to Michigan after she finished high school to be close to her cousin. The view from Amanda's upstairs master bed room window was breath taking. She would sit there for hours when she wanted to just relax after a hectic day at work.

Amanda loved her job as a 911 emergency operator and making good money but not enough to live the life style she was used to living with her parents and now with Gunnar if she was to leave. Gunnar took an early retirement and was still working. He was getting a pension check and annuity check every month and an employment check. He paid all the bills and only asked that Amanda keep the house clean, do the laundry, and the cooking, all the wifely duties. He also demanded her not to gain weight and only wear night gowns to bed at night and no pajamas.  And for sixteen years Amanda did just that except for the weight gain.

In the sixteen years Gunnar and Amanda been together Amanda gained seventy pounds. Gunnar told her if she lose the weight that he would marry her. Amanda spent thousands of dollars trying to lose the extra weight only to gain more so she just gave up. Gunnar never looked at Amanda the same anymore, he never gave her that little pat when they pass each other, they never kissed goodnight anymore and their love making was down to zero.

Amanda wanted to lose the weight but she was too depressed. She knew when Gunnar wasn't home or at work he was at Traci's his ex-girlfriend's visiting the boy's and when the boy's came to visit him at their house they barley breathed one word to her. They would say, dad why is Amanda wearing your house shoes? Don't she have her own? Or did Amanda go to work today or they would ask what did Amanda cook today? They knew she came home and cooked every day or they would ask, have Amanda made that pepper chicken again? Not even looking at her sitting in the same room. No she hasn't their dad would respond maybe I can get her to make you some this week he smiled turning to look at Amanda who was getting up to leave the room, no one was talking to her anyway so she would go  see what rerun was playing on Life Time.

Their fourteen and fifteen year old daughters were visiting friends, if they knew their two older brothers were there they would rush right home to see them. They loved their older brothers very much. Gunnar Jr. was a senior in high school and Major was a junior, Kendra was a sophomore and Madison was in the eighth grade after failing a year which Gunnar blamed on Amanda.

Gunnar's boys were tall and slim like their mom Traci and his girls were short and chubby like Amanda after she lost her shape. Amanda knew Traci and Gunnar were sleeping together because when Gunnar took his son to Maryland to visit his future college, Traci went with them and she know they stayed in the same hotel room but Gunnar never admitted it. When Traci bring the boy's over to visit their dad Amanda notice she always hug Gummer a little too long. You know Gun is going to need a car next year when he goes to college Traci told Gunnar. Yes I know, Gunnar told her I was thinking about giving him Amanda's car and buying her a new one.

Amanda just sat and listened while they talked thinking "I just got that car last year and why he didn't discuss it with me first." Amanda liked Gunnar Jr. Who they called Gun and Major but the only thing she didn't like about them was the only time they came over to visit their father was when they needed money, even though their dad paid child support every month, bought all their clothes, shoes, paid their basketball fees for school, basketball uniforms, food when Major told him that they didn't have any food in the house. He bought them an entire house full of furniture including washer, dryer, refrigerator, stove living room furniture because Traci denounced the boy's tore up the other furniture. He even bought a patio set for outside because Traci insisted they needed it, she didn't need a boyfriend because she could always count on Gunnar.

Gunnar never chastised the boy's when they exhibited bad behavior or made bad choices. What he didn't know was that he was making the situation worse because he was protecting them from the consequences of their actions. But he loved them and the problem with that is he was helping to enable them instead of helping them. But his daughters were his pride and joy, they got the same privilege as the boy's, and more, he wouldn't let Amanda chastise them because his daughters could do no wrong.

Traci and Gunnar separated when the boys were one and two, then he met Amanda they had Kendra and one year later Madison. Gunnar had four kids in four years all one year apart. Gunnar started working at the Social Security Administration Office right out of high school and after working there for twenty eight years he took an early retirement then after six months he got bored and went back. Now he still gets his pension, annuity check, and employment check, so money was no problem for him. Amanda was able to shop at her leisure Gunnar never gave her a limit, and

Amanda never took advantage of the situation. They took two weeks vacations four times a year.

Kendra had a boyfriend name Kevin Richardson. Kevin was in her geometry class and according to Kendra the most handsome boy at school. Most days Kendra would just sit in the lunchroom with her lunch getting cold in front of her on the tray. She would have her geometry book opened and her head down. Then one day Kevin decided to ask her if she needed help in geometry because he was passing the class with "A's". After three weeks Kendra finally got it. Now do me a favor and start eating your lunch Kevin told her. For the next two months when you saw one you saw the other. Kendra hated when she had to go on vacation with her family and leave Kevin.

When she first came home and asked her mom if she could have a boyfriend she told her it was something she had to talk over with Gunnar. That evening when Gunnar came home Kendra was nervous she waited until after he ate dinner then she asked him. I would have to meet him first Gunnar told his daughter I can call him now Kendra said. When Kevin arrived he was very nervous Gunnar took him into the study closed the door and gave him the talk only two words "no sex" from the look on Gunnar's face Kevin knew he was serious. Amanda had seen her daughter and Kevin doing some heavy kissing on the front porch one night after returning from the movies and hope that's as far as they went. Gunnar Jr. on the other hand had plenty of girlfriends. Amanda even saw when the condom pack fell out of his coat pocket but she never told his dad.

Officer Anthony Stevin Moore never missed the opportunity to go to the station because he knew he was going to see Amanda. On his way out Anthony would always walk into the communications room and everyone knew why he was there. Amanda knew Anthony was married and had a daughter JJ away in college and his wife Tiffany twelve years his junior was a secretary for a big time lawyer and they lived in a big beautiful home on the North side which Amanda never saw.

Amanda knew Anthony was fond of her and she was fond of him also, she liked that bad boy swag about him. For the first year and a half they would just talk when he came to the station, Anthony would always make Amanda blush, he was so good looking. One day when Anthony came to see her he noticed she wasn't the same. Is anything wrong he inquired? Things aren't going well at home Amanda calmed, let's have lunch and talk about it Anthony offered.

Anthony made her feel like a girl again, she never smiled until she was with him she never told anyone about Anthony even Charlotte, but she had a feeling that everyone at work knew because of the way she looked at him when he walked into the communications room. Anthony and Amanda would schedule their lunch breaks at the same time and meet at the little cafe across the street from the first district police department where she worked which they now called their place.

Some times their lunch would be interrupted if an emergency came up and Anthony had to leave, leaving his food untouched sometimes. It first started out with lunch then the kissing started Amanda missed kissing and then the touching started and one day Anthony asked Amanda if he could take her to the hotel and as bad as Amanda wanted to go she had to tell him no.

Amanda knew Anthony couldn't take care of her like Gunnar did and plus he had a real family, a wife and daughter something Amanda always wanted. Gunnar would always say it's only a piece of paper, we live together anyway. But Amanda wanted more, she "wanted" that piece of paper saying that they belong to each other until death but after sixteen years she doubted if she would ever get it. Charlotte always preached that she would be going to her daughter's and his son's wedding still unmarried.

Seven months later it happened, Traci called and demanded her and the boys were on their way over and they needed to talk. When they arrived at Gunnar and Amanda's it wasn't like their usual visit they didn't need money this time. Gunnar Jr.'s girlfriend, Dominique Clark was pregnant and he wanted to marry her before the baby comes. What about college son his dad moaned? It's all set and you are supposed to be leaving in six months after you graduate.

I'll go to a local college Gunnar Jr. argued. But Gun
you'll be throwing your whole future away Traci cried.
I don't care Gunnar Jr. argued, I love her. "You're only
seventeen, you don't know what love is yet." Traci
shouted a little too loud with her hands on her hips.
Yes I do mom I love Dom and she loves me and we
will get married if you like it or not. "No you're not",
Gunnar Sr. spoke up. Gunnar Jr. hit the table turning
over their coffee and stormed out.

Someone needs to stop him Amanda spoke up as she
went to get a towel to clean up the mess he just made.
Traci left and found her son sitting in the car
steaming. When Traci sat in the car Gunnar spoke up,
mom don't try to talk me out of it Dominique and I
are getting married and that's it. But son you're not
being sensible Traci breathed as she drove them back
home. If you love her and she loves you why don't the
two of you wait until after school and then think about
getting married? Because we only have nine months
before the baby comes Gunnar told her.

Yes and about the baby Traci persisted, who's going to
take care of the baby? I am Gunnar said, oh do you
have a job Traci indicated? No but you do he wined
and you get a check from dad every month for us.
That's to help keep a roof over you and your brothers'
head. Well the baby is a part of me and I'll share my
part of the roof with him Gunnar said groaning. Traci
saw she was getting nowhere with Gunnar at this time
she wanted to reach out to Dominique's mom and see

if they could work together to talk about the kids to let them know this is not a good time to get married.

The following week Traci met up with Dominique's mom and explained to her that Gunnar had everything all set up for him to leave for college in six months which was already paid for, for the first year and his dad was getting him a car and that his life was on track but if he was to marry her daughter that would destroy everything. Then to Traci's surprise Patricia Clark blew up "What the hell do you mean your son? I don't give a damn about your son 'my daughter is the one that's pregnant what about her' what about her future Miss. "Traci?" My daughter didn't get pregnant by herself you know.

I know Traci gasped still in shock the conversation wasn't going the way she expected. She thought her and Miss. Clark would sit down over coffee and straighten the whole thing out like two adults but Dominique's mom was scaring the hell out of her and all she could think about was running out of there. When Patricia Clark finally calmed down Traci saw her exit to leave and told her maybe this was not a good time.

When Traci got back in the car her hands were shaking she passed a pub and decided to stop in for a drink to calm her nerves. While sitting at the bar drinking a Michelob berried in her own thoughts she had a feeling that someone was starring at her. When she looked around she saw a gentleman two seats over starring at her. Another Michelob for the lady he told the bartender. He walked over to Traci and introduced himself as Marcus.

Thank you for the drink Traci told him when the bartender placed the beer on the bar in front of her. Are you having a bad day like me Traci asked him? Yes, and by the way what's you name Marcus asked her? I'm Traci and I wish I could start this day all over again. Well let's see who's having the worse day Marcus told her. You first, no you go first Traci told him drinking the last of her first Michelob. Well Marcus started off I've worked at my job for thirty some years now and my supervisor is retiring next month and word had been going around the office that I was getting his position so for the last two weeks I have been walking around with my chest stuck out acting like a big shot with a smile on my face, then this morning when the boss called me into his office I thought this was going to be the day.

When I entered his office he asked me what I felt about Margaret a girl that was hired two weeks ago right out of college. I really laid on the compliments about Margaret because I thought she was smart, she knew her work, she caught on fast and her work was magnificent. Well I'm thinking about giving her the supervisor position my boss said and it took all my strength to keeps my posture siting in the chair. When I left his office I told my supervisor I wasn't well and needed to go home, and here I am Marcus said.

Wow Traci told him touching his hand on the bar. So what's your story little lady Marcus asked Traci. Well

Traci started my teenage son just informed us his girlfriend is pregnant. Ouch Marcus said. It gets worse Traci told him I just tried to talk to her mother telling her our son will be going to college this year and couldn't afford a baby and she practically cursed me out and spit in my face. I think you and your husband should stay out of it Marcus told her let them handle it or you will lose them but be there for them when they fall. We're not married Traci told him, this brought a smile to Marcus face. Traci and Marcus talked for another hour and exchanged phone numbers.

On the drive home she called Gunnar Sr. and told him about the conversation with Dominique's mom. I'll talk to Gunnar again he told her. Gunnar called his son on his cell phone and he picked up on the first ring and started out with dad I need fifteen hundred dollars. Sure son his dad answered thinking his son and Dominique had finally come to their senses. Gunnar took the bus to his dad and got the money not telling him what he needed it for but his dad just knew it was to take care of their little problem. Gunnar called Traci back to tell her that everything was taking care of. Traci wanted to come over and talk but Gunnar told her not tonight Kendra was bringing her boyfriend's parents over to meet them. So is she pregnant too Traci said? Bye Traci, Gunnar protested and hung up without responding to her little comment.

Amanda was in the kitchen fixing baked chicken, mashed potatoes, string beans and a chocolate cake for desert. Charlotte was making a large pan of cornbread for her because Amanda never learned how to make good cornbread. Madison came down stairs three times wearing different outfits to get her mom's approval, what about this one Madison said? The third time she came down Charlotte had arrived with the pan of cornbread and Madison ran to her "hi" cousin Charlotte, hey baby girl Charlotte said giving her a big hug. Why do you always call me baby girl I'm not a baby anymore. "Sorry" it's a habit Charlotte said.

The day you were born I came to see you and you looked like a baby doll and ever since then I have called you baby girl "Oh and I love the outfit." Thanks Madison sung, can I just go with you and skip the dinner? No I think your sister wants you here Charlotte said why don't you and I catch a movie next Saturday morning? Ok Madison squealed bouncing out the kitchen. Didn't forget next Saturday I'm sure you won't let me Charlotte shouted back.

Amanda told Charlotte Gunnar dropped the kids off at the movies and Kevin's parents will pick them up and bring them here for dinner. Are you nervous Charlotte asked? No their just kids it's not like their getting married.  Oh I went to see that new play last night Charlotte said and I think you should go see it, it was so good. Really who did you go with Amanda asked? Just a friend from work Charlotte blushed. Are you blushing Amanda asked? No, oh yes I think you are Amanda said. What's his name? Big Mike Charlotte said. Big Mike Amanda said, what kind of name is that?  Well he has a son name Mike so that's why they call him big Mike.

When the kids returned from the movies they came bouncing into the house holding hands with Kevin's parents following behind them. Dad this is Kevin's parents Mr. and Mrs. Richardson. Gunnar then saw where Kevin got his curly fine hair and saucer eyes. It really smells good in here Mr. Richardson said smelling the aroma inside the house. I hope you like chicken Madison spoke up.  Vincent Richardson he said extending his hand to Gunnar. Gunnar led the group into the den and while following him Mrs. Richardson noticed the beautiful living room and dining room where the table was set with beautiful pink china.

After they were all seated in the cozy den Gunnar offered everyone drinks. You have a beautiful home Mr. Richardson said, thank you Kendra responded. Mr. Richardson sat in the big comfortable chair by the fire place which was lit and putting out good heat. Mrs. Richardson, Gunnar and Kendra sat on the couch, Madison sat on the love seat and Kevin sat in the second chair in the room. The conversation in the room went well and they all agreed on the same thing. I think we have pretty smart children Mr. Richardson said I know they will make good decisions all the time he was looking at Kevin, remember school is the most important thing here, school comes first "Yes Sir" Kevin said, and swallowed hard.

Amanda entered the room and took the seat on the love seat next to Madison. Mom this is Kevin's mom Mrs. Richardson, Kendra said. It is so nice to finally meet you Amanda told her. And this is Mr. Richardson Kevin's dad, Amanda turned her attention to the other side of the room and froze, she had only seconds to gain her composure. He also had that same expression on his face. It's nice to meet you Amanda said trying to sound professional but her insides were screaming. Amanda excused herself and left the room by the time she reached the kitchen she was shaking all over. She used the kitchen phone to call Charlotte and dropped the phone three times before completing the call.

"No" Charlotte said. When did he move to Michigan? I don't know Amanda told her shaking from head to toe, but he's in our den drinking wine with my family. You need to get yourself together, no one knows but you and him. Amanda Marie Collins Don't you dare ruin this evening for Kendra now you hang up this phone and get your ass back in there and act normal. What's that noise Amanda asked? Big Mike and I are at a bar she told her. Amanda hung up the phone and went back into the den and said dinner was ready.

Kendra and Kevin held hands on the way to the dining room. Earlier Gunnar took one of the leaves out of the table that sat twelve to accommodate eight and put the other four chairs away. The conversation over dinner went better than they expected. The kids told them what they were doing in school and about their teachers. Gunnar and Amanda was glad that everyone was on the same page, they were just two teenagers in love and happy with each other's company.

Amanda noticed the glow in her daughters' eyes when she looked at Kevin across the table and remembered when she looked at Gunnar that same way sixteen years ago. He told her she was the most beautiful girl he had ever seen and they couldn't keep their hands off each other. Never got tired of each other they wanted to be with each other twenty four hours a day seven days a week.

Then Amanda got too comfortable and the weight started coming on, that's when Gunnar stopped looking at her the same way. Amanda didn't notice until after the girls were born that the weight was not coming off after each pregnancy. That's when she started spending thousands of dollars trying to get it off. She joined gyms, weight loss centers, ate disgusting foods, starved herself, did body wrap, and then thought about liposuction until Charlotte talked her out of it saying it was dangerous.

Then Amanda got frustrated and cried a lot and the more she cried the more she ate. What's for desert Kendra said jarring her mom's thoughts back to the present time. Oh I made chocolate cake Amanda said your favorite. I'll get it Kendra said getting up and going into the kitchen. Amanda was glad her and Vincent was sitting on the same side of the table that way she didn't have to make eye contact with him. Over cake they all talked about the kid's college.

Gunnar told the Richardson's that Kendra started writing letters to colleges in the seventh grade and she must have sent out a hundred letters and so far had gotten about twenty five back and they were still coming at least one a month from different colleges that she kept in a shoe box under her bed. Kevin just started writing to colleges last week when Kendra told him he had to Mr. Richardson said. I didn't know having my first girlfriend at fifteen would be so demanding Kevin laughed. Kendra helped him write the letters, she always knew Kevin wanted to be a special education teacher and she always wanted to be a high school counselor.

Wouldn't it be nice if we worked at the same school Kendra said? Amanda, Gunnar and Kendra walked the Richardson's out to their car and Vincent put his index finger to his lip for Amanda to see and she gave him a nod and they all promised to stay in touch.

Two weeks later all was going good Gunnar had not heard from Traci or the boy's no news is good news he told himself. Until that evening at dinner Kendra told her dad that her friend Sonya has a friend that goes to the same high school Gunnar Jr. goes to and Sonya's friend said that Dominique is going around showing off a ring she says Gunnar bought for her and that they are getting married.

"What?" her dad said, are you serious? What exactly did this Sonya say? She said that Dominique is wearing a wedding band and showing it off to all the girls and telling them her and my brother is getting married. Are you sure they're talking about Dominique Clark? Yes dad Kendra said reluctantly. "Oh no he's not" Gunnar said getting up from the table and leaving the room. They could hear him on the phone in the den talking to Gunnar Jr. and he was shouting into the phone. He's never going to speak to you again Madison said to her sister and stormed out leaving her plate only half empty. You did the right thing Amanda told her daughter, thanks mom but why do I feel so bad.

Kendra stayed behind to help her mom clear the table and clean the kitchen. They could still hear Gunnar on the phone talking very loudly to Gunnar Jr. While Kendra stacked the dishwasher she asked her mom do you think Gunnar Jr. Will be mad at me for telling dad? Its ok honey Amanda said sometimes you have to speak up so no one gets hurt in the end. He will be mad for a while but it won't be forever. Kendra gave her mom a peck on the cheek and said thanks mom and went up to her room to call Kevin. Amanda sat at the kitchen table and wondered what Anthony was doing he hadn't come into the station today and she found herself missing him.

It was Anthony's day off and he met with two other officers at the pool hall and shot three games of pool winning only one. Then the threesome went to I-hop for a bite to eat, when the manager noticed they were cops he told them their meal was on the house. After they finished one of the officers said he had a lot of things to fix around the house and had to get home and do them because he was tired of hearing his wife's mouth. The other officer said he had to pick his son up from school early for a dentist appointment.

Anthony said I'm sure my wife has something at home for me to do also. So they all said their goodbyes and went their separate ways. At home Anthony found a note on the refrigerator saying: "the upstairs sink is leaking again, the dryer is not getting hot as it used to. Oh and the lock on the front screen door is lose". After reading the note Anthony looked at the clock and thought about calling Amanda at work but didn't think it was a good idea.

Instead he took an hour nap and then started on the list of things his wife left for him to do. When Mrs. Moore returned home that evening Anthony had gotten his tool box out the garage and had fixed the leaky sink up stairs, he had to take the bottom panel of the dryer off and go to the hardware store to buy a part, came back home and fixed it now it was working like new, then he tightened the lock on the front screen door and started dinner.

The next morning after roll call Anthony went to the communication room to say hi to Amanda. Are we on for lunch today he asked her? Yes Amanda said well I'll see you there. That afternoon Amanda waited for an hour for Anthony at the cafe but he never showed. When she walked back across the street and to her station she saw everyone was franticly talking on the phones and the radio, dispatch was yelling out orders and the 911 operators were shouting back "another officer down" Amanda got scared. The 911 operator next to her was still taking 911 calls about the officers being down in a shoot-out and In between calls she filled Amanda in on what was going on.

There was a traffic stop and when the officer got out his patrol car the man in the other car started shooting. A citizen saw the whole thing and called 911 saying a police officer had just got shot and was laying in the street. When dispatch was given the information there were already six police cars chasing this guy and every car that came close to him he would fire at them they flattened two of his tires and the driver was still doing eighty. Then Amanda heard on the dispatch radio "suspect down" we got that son of a bitch.

She left her station and walked to the dispatch station and asked about the officers that were shot. The son of a bitch got three of our officers the dispatch was shouting. Do we have names yet Amanda asked? Not yet the dispatch yelled back. Amanda walked back to her desk shaking. When 3:00 came Amanda's shift was over but she did not want to go home without knowing the names of the officers that had got shot. It was Wednesday and she was off the next two days, her schedule alternated, Monday and Tuesday off then the next week Tuesday and Wednesday off, then Wednesday and Thursday off then the next week.

She could not leave that station and sit at home for two days without knowing something. She tried Anthony's cell phone, no answer, maybe he's in a dead zone, she waited one minute and tried again, still no answer. She couldn't wait until she got home and find out that he was hurt or even killed she had to know now. She tried his number four more times still no answer. She drove crying the whole hour drive home but this day it took two hours because she had trouble seeing the road through her tears.

When she got home she tried him again but still no answer. She noticed her eyes were red and when Gunnar came home she was a nervous wreck and lying in bed saying she had a hard day at work. You just stay in bed Gunnar said I'll feed the girls, can I get you anything he asked her? "No thanks", Amanda said, "just take care of the girls". Amanda turned over and closed her eyes and when she opened them again the room was dark and the clock on her night stand said 8:00 she got up and went to the master bed rooms sitting room, sat on the couch and turned the TV on to watch the 8:00 news. When she turned it on they were already talking about the police offer's that had been shoot and they had already lost two and the third one Officer Isadore Williams was in critical condition and had half the police department at his bed side.

"What's the name of the officer's that was shot Amanda was shouting to the TV screen and as she was saying it the news announcer was saying the names, unfortunately officer Mike Cadenza and Vincent McMillon were the unfortunate ones. Then the camera crew ran to Anthony coming out of the front

doors of the hospital they wanted to interview
Anthony. We are standing here with Officer Anthony
Stevin Moore best friends with Vincent McMillian.
"He's alive" Amanda said to the TV with tears rolling
down her face. Can you give us an update on Officer
Isadore Williams the reporter was asking Anthony
sticking a microphone in his face? Officer Williams is
still in critical condition but thanks to his bullet proof
vest the doctors think he will make a full recovery.
What about the families of the deceased, how are they
handling this? No more questions Anthony was saying
holding his hand up walking away from the reporters
but they followed him all the way to his car still asking
questions.

Amanda took a chance and sent him a text message
simply saying "hi, glad you're ok." He answered her
text right away saying "busy all day, see you
tomorrow" she texted back "off tomorrow but I'll drive
to the cafe at twelve. She was deleting the text when
Madison walked in. Hi mommy are you feeling better,
she came in to her give her mom a hug? I am now her
mom said, your hair smells like strawberries Amanda
told her. It's the new shampoo that you bought for me
remember? Oh yes I remember Amanda said I'm
sorry I've had so much on my mind lately.

Its ok mommy Madison said I'm just glad you're
feeling better now. Do you know what Alisa Rashaan
did today? No what did Alisa Rashaan do today?
Amanda said. In civic class we have to do an hour a
week civic duty Madison said and last week Alisa

worked in the attendance office and while she was working there she saw Mrs. Green's test that she give every year with the answer key. She wrote all the answers down and shared them with Billy Graves and today when Mrs. Green gave the test Alisa got all the answers wrong and Billy Graves got all his answers right. Alisa didn't know there was an A&B test with the same questions but in different order and an A&B answer key.

So the answers she wrote down were the answers to test B which Billy took and not hers. So Mrs. Graves has to come up to school tomorrow and I think Alisa and Billy is going to be in a lot of trouble. And last year when we were in seventh grade Billy got into trouble a lot too. Once he pulled Katherine Collins hair and made her cry he sat behind her in math class and Katherine wouldn't give him the answer to number six so Billy pulled her hair really hard and Katherine cried out. Mrs. Pelletier the math teacher sent Billy to the office and sent Katherine to the nurse because she wouldn't stop crying. Mrs. Graves and Mrs. Collins came up to the school and Billy was suspended and Mrs. Collins took Katherine home because she said her head hurt.

When Billy returned back to school three days later he apologized to Katherine and said his mom was upset because she had to take a day off her new job at the daycare where she had only worked two weeks. Billy's baby brother Alex has started kindergarten and Mrs. Graves needed something to do during the day so she got a job at the daycare. The bus would drop Alex off at the daycare then they would go home to wait for Billy's bus to bring him home.

Gunnar was standing in the doorway and told his daughter "I don't want you hanging around this Billy kid" he sounds like trouble. I don't hang around him dad Madison said he's just in one of my classes. That's my girl Gunnar said and walked over and given his daughter a kiss on the top of her head. Your hair smells good he told her then he turned to Amanda are you feeling better?

Yes Amanda said I guess I had a rough day at work. I couldn't do your job Gunnar told her, you have to listen to people's problems for eight hours. Actually it's only six Amanda said we get an hour lunch break and two thirty minutes breaks, they thought we would need the two breaks after all the stressful emergency calls. So maybe I'll come and take you to lunch one day Gunnar said with a big smile on his face but Amanda wasn't smiling. Come on Mad let's let mom get some rest. Can we have ice cream Madison was asking her dad as they left the room?

Kendra was in her room lying across her bed talking to Kevin on the phone. I'm going to have to buy more stamps he was saying. I know, when I was writing my letters my mom and dad got tired of me saying I need more stamps. Why can't I just e-mail them? "No" Kendra said this is more personal and they know you really want it.

Gunnar had not heard from his son in a couple of weeks and wanted to wait a while until both of them had time to cool down. The following Saturday when he woke he decided he would call his son and try talking to him again. He wanted to know why he bought Dominique a ring with the money he gave him. He took a long stretch and thought he would have a cup of coffee before he made the call. He got out of bed and headed for the bathroom when his cell phone on the dresser started to ring. He picked it up and looked at the caller ID, it was Traci. He looked back at the clock on the night sand it was only eight fifty. What could Traci want this early in the morning? He didn't feel like talking to her right now.

Gunnar put the phone back down and continued on to the bathroom and when he came out the home phone was ringing and then he heard Amanda calling up to him "Gunnar its Traci she's crying and she says it's important. Gunnar sat on the side of the bed and picked up the phone. Before he could get the phone to his ear he heard Traci crying. What happened Gunnar spouted into the phone? Are the boy's ok? Why did you give Gunnar money to buy Dominique a ring Traci shouted back? I didn't Gunnar said, he said he needed the money, I thought they had come to their senses and I was happy to give Him the money. Well that's what you get for thinking Traci shouted back now we have a daughter in law. "What?" Gunnar said. You heard me they got married last night. Where are they Gunnar demanded? In my living room sitting on the couch like their at home, but they're not staying here.

Put him on the phone Gunnar said "No, you get your ass over here" Traci said I'm not raising a married man, and I'm defiantly not raising no baby. Gunnar Jr. heard his mom shouting on the phone to his dad and came into her bedroom. You don't have to worry about us mom we will be staying with Dominique's mom, she said we can stay until the baby comes. "What about school Gunnar?" Traci screamed at her son, I'm not thinking about no baby. I'm thinking about your education but you can't understand what we are trying to tell you, your problem is you think you're grown but you're still a kid and now you have went and messed up your whole life.

Dominique rushed into Traci's bedroom and stood at the door saying "I don't appreciate you talking to my husband in that tone" "What the hell" Traci said and then the phone went dead on Gunnar's end. He threw on jeans and a sweatshirt then ran down the stairs hollering to Amanda at the back door as he put his feet into his boots with no socks, I'm going to Traci's we have a crisis and before Amanda could say anything he was out the door. Gunnar ran two red lights before he pulled up in front of Traci's house leaving one wheel up on the curb he ran up the front stairs taking them two at a time. He rushed into the house without ringing the bell and Traci, Gunnar Jr. And Dominique could be heard from the front of the house.

He followed their voices back to Traci's bedroom. You really need to keep it down before the neighbors call the police Gunnar shouted. Let's all sit down and talk this thing out like adults. Gunnar guided them all to the kitchen and when they were all seated everyone started talking at once. Then Gunnar hit the glass table and cracked the glass, which got everyone's attention. I'll buy you another one he said to Traci when he seen the expression on her face. Now let's talk about this marriage, Dominique and I was married yesterday his son spoke up. I told you we were going to get married it's not like we didn't tell you and you even gave me the money for the ring and the justice of the piece dad. "When you asked me for that money I thought you were going to pay a doctor to take care of your little problem his dad shouted," and what problem would that be dad?

You know exactly what I'm talking about Gunnar said getting angry. No why don't you tell us what our problem is Gunnar Jr. said. How could you say that about your own grandson Dominique cried? You know exactly what I thought the money was for Gunnar Sr. said I even called your mom and told her it was all settled. Well you were wrong his son said. Well what about school? Dominique and I will finish school. And what about college Traci said, I will have to give up my tuition in Maryland and go to a local college here in Michigan her son said. And who's going to pay for it Traci said. I'll get a job and pay for it myself if I have to Gunnar said.

Come on let's go Dominique said getting up from the table, I'm tired. I just need to pack a few things Gunnar Jr. said and left the kitchen. When he came down with two large suit cases he told his mom he would return the suit cases tomorrow. I'll drive you two over his dad said. On the drive to Dominique's house Gunnar asked his dad if they could stop at McDonalds. Didn't the doctor put you on a special diet he asked Dominique and start you on vitamins? Yes but its ok if I have Big Mac with extra pickles, fries and a chocolate shake Dominique said.

While Gunnar was out Amanda called to check on officer Isadore Williams at Mercy hospital. Her call was switched to the nursing station on his floor, he's still holding on the nurse said we think he will make a full recovery but it's going to take some time. He has a visitor right now but I can transfer your call to his room. "Oh no," Amanda said, I don't want to interrupt him, I know his wife is going through a lot right now, no it's not his wife it's his fellow officer Mr. Moore. Ok you can transfer me Amanda said in a sweet voice. She was surprised when Anthony answered the phone in Isadora's room.

Officer Moore he said into the receiver, good morning officer Moore Amanda said I'm calling to check on officer Isadore, how is he? Amanda said. He has a long way to go Anthony said but I told him if he don't fight to get better that I was going to kick his ass. Amanda laughed at the order Anthony gave Isadore and what did he say to that she said, he gave me the thumbs up.

How have you been Anthony asked? I'm fine now, I mean I'm upset that we lost some of our officer's and about Isadore but I'm glad you're safe. So what are you doing on your day off Antony asked? We have a crisis over at Gunnar's ex with one of the boy's. He rushed out of here about two hours ago so I think it's something serious. Well the radio has been quiet for the last two hours Anthony told her, no one has called the police, they both laughed. Do you want to meet for lunch? I'll see you at our place about one Amanda said, ok Anthony said and hung up.

  When Gunnar got to Dominique's moms house he helped his son carry the two oversized bags inside. Dominique's mom told him where to put the bags. If we can do anything to help Gunnar Sr. said, doctor bills, transportation to the doctor appointments, groceries' please just give us a call. It was kind of you to take them in. "Oh don't you worry" Patricia Clark said don't you think for one minute that I'm going to take care of your son and his wife by myself. But his wife is your daughter, Gunnar shot back in the same voice. Yes, but she's married now and she's not my responsibility any more. She's his wife now and he's responsible for her now. I'm just giving them a place to stay for nine months.

Well like I said call if you need anything Gunnar has the number. You people with a little money think you could just pay your way out of everything and the little people should bow at your feet well I'll tell you one thing Patricia  hissed you may as well be ready to dig deep in those pockets of yours because I'm not going to go without. I will live my life the same way I've always have I'm not going to sacrifice the things that I need to take care of them. I'll get a job Gunnar Jr. spoke up, then Dominique's mom turned on him. You're seventeen what kind of job can you get besides a job at a fast food restaurant. And don't you think for one minute you're going to Maryland in six months and leaving your wife and unborn child here. "Mom" Dominique said with tears in her eyes.

Amanda went upstairs to shower and get dressed when she came back down at eleven forty five, Gunnar was sitting on the couch with his face in his hands. "You look nice," he told Amanda and you smell wonderful, "thank you," Amanda said. Where might you be off to Gunnar asked her? First of all what happened this morning she asked him. Gunnar and Amanda got married last night, "No they didn't" Amanda said shocked.

Where will they be staying she asked? With Dominique's mom and she's not too happy about it either. But he's supposed to be leaving in two months for college. Now he wants to stay here and go to the local college. "Wow" I think if he stays in Michigan he won't go to college. Yes I do too Gunnar said. I don't know what to do now. Dominique's mom don't really want them there and Traci don't want Dominique there. They made their decision without thinking everything out and now they're stuck, Amanda preached. They're just kids Gunnar said, so what now Amanda said, I told Dominique's mom that I would help out as much as I can. It seems that we are the only ones with a stable family foundation. So what are you saying Amanda questioned? Her mom said they could only stay there for nine months so they may have to come here after the baby is born. Gunnar saw the disappointed look on Amanda's face and she didn't try to hide it. After fifteen minutes they were still talking and Amanda look down at her watch it was twelve fifteen. She didn't feel like going to lunch now, not even Anthony could cheer her up.

Kendra came rushing down the stairs and saw her mom and dad sitting on the couch in serious thought. Hey guess what? They both turned around looking at her relieved to have some good news in the mist of the bad. Kevin got his first letter today and they said that they will consider him for the scholarship. Why are you all dressed up mom Kendra asked? I was going to meet Charlotte for lunch but now I don't feel like going. You can take me to lunch Kendra said. I want to go too Madison said coming into the room.

Why don't you girls go and have lunch and just bring me something back Gunnar said. The girls wanted different foods, Madison wanted Chinese and Kendra wanted Mandarin so Amanda decided on steak. They went to Out Back Steak House and all three enjoyed their meal. Amanda had T-bone with baked potato and salad, Kendra ordered the rib eye with baked

sweet potato and corn on the cob and Madison
ordered the sirloin steak patty on a bun with fries and
baked apples. They all tasted each other's food then
Amanda decided to tell them about their brother. I
was hoping he didn't marry her Kendra said I've heard
some bad things about her.

Well there's nothing we can do now Amanda said they
got married last night. Then Amanda got a text, when
she looked at her phone Anthony had left her a
message saying sorry I missed you something must
have come up and that he was on his way to the
hospital to visit Isadore. Amanda just texted back
"ok."

The rest of their lunch went well Madison made them
laugh telling them things that Billy Graves did at
school. I think he gets in trouble all the time because
he loves the attention he gets from us Madison said.
We always give him the biggest laugh when he do
stupid things and the longer we laugh the more he
does. So actually you all are edging him on Kendra
said and that's not right. Well yes I guess so Madison
said. The next time Billy does something bad why
don't you be the one to tell him it's wrong and he
shouldn't do it her mom said. Ok mom I'll try it but it
may ruin his reputation, they all laughed.

Back at home Gunnar tried to take a nap but his brain
was running like a motor. He called Traci to tell her
what happened when he dropped the kids off. What
are we going to do she asked him. I don't know Tra,
you haven't called me Tra in years. I know it's been a

while Gunnar said. When are you going out of town again Traci teased, I don't know but I'll let you know when I do.

So I guess Gun won't be going on the next cruse with us Gunnar said, so I guess it will just be Amanda, the girls, Major and me. It's going to be strange going on vacation without him. Are you scared Traci whispered? About what Gunnar said? Having our first grandchild. Not really I just wish it would have all been different and Gunnar would have listened to us and did it our way. Who's to say they will continue school now that they think their grown. Where did we go wrong with that boy Traci cried? He's going to still need our help you know, yes I know Traci replied.

Do you think I was too harsh toward them she asked, just a little Gunnar laughed. He was still laughing when Amanda and his daughter's walked in. We'll talk soon he said and hung up the phone. Who was on the phone Amanda asked? It was Traci, Gunnar said. What was so funny Amanda said, we were just laughing about the fact that we will be grandparents in nine months. Did you bring me anything Gunnar asked? Yes, Madison is bringing it in Amanda said and went upstairs. Kendra went to her room to call Kevin and Morgan stayed down stairs to talk to her dad while he ate his take out lunch and then they watched an old movie on TV.

At seven that evening Gunnar said he was putting burgers on the grill and would somebody make a big salad. Don't cook any for me Kendra said, Kevin's mom is coming to pick me up and I'm eating dinner over there. Don't stay to late honey Amanda told her. I won't mom, I think their cooking burgers on the grill too because when I was talking to Kevin earlier he said he had to clean the grill. Amanda and Madison made a big salad while Gunnar mixed the seasoning into the ground beef and he also cut up a small onion and garlic to add to his mix. "OK girls, burgers will be ready in ten minutes." Gunnar sang as he exited the patio door.

Dad sure is in a good mood Kendra smiled, then she heard a horn out front and yelled bye to her mom while running out the door. Gunnar, Madison and Amanda sat eating their burgers and salad when Gunnar asked her how her aunt was. Aunt Susan is doing great her body shows no sign of the cancer and Charlotte and her goes to church every Sunday and she loves singing in the choir. Can we invite them to dinner sometime Madison asked?

We sure can pumpkin Amanda smiled at her daughter. Grandma and grandpa said they're going to come to my graduation Madison told her parent's, and I might go back to New York with them for a couple of weeks. After the burgers Gunnar asked them if they wanted to go out for ice cream. "Not me," Amanda replied, I think I'll pass too, "Madison said, "but if you go just get me pistachio and I'll eat it later".

Madison helped her mom clean the kitchen while Gunnar went into his office and closed the door. After the kitchen was clean Madison went to her room to get on her computer and Amanda sat in her window set in the master bed room looking out. She was still sitting there when Kevin walked Kendra up the front stairs to the front door and gave her a very long kiss before running back to the car to join his dad.

When Gunnar came to bed that night he asked Amanda did she know Frank and Jonnie was coming for the graduation? Well they are my parents she said. I know Gunnar said it's just that I know they don't like your living arrangement and I want them to feel comfortable in our home. Then he slid into bed and put his arm around Amanda something he hadn't done in years. Who are you she asked? I know it's been a while so what do you think? About what Amanda laughed?

I can show you better than I can tell you Gunnar said turning off the light. The next morning they made love again before they got up to go to work. Amanda got up first and started the shower and Gunnar joined her in the shower, once more for the road he said? Amanda went to work with a smile on her face and feeling fantastic. She had forgot she was having lunch with Anthony at the cafe at twelve. It was eleven twenty-five when her cell phone rang and she looked at the ID and seen Gunnar's name and smiled. Gunnar asked her if she wanted to meet somewhere for lunch, sure that would be nice Amanda said.

I noticed a little cafe across the street from the precinct did you want to meet there Gunnar asked. No I think I have a taste for Chinese Amanda said, thinking fast. Ok, I know a place not too far from your job, meet me out front at twelve and I'll have you back by one. After she pushed the disconnect button she remembered her lunch date with Anthony. As she got ready to call him he appeared at her station. I was just getting ready to call you she said looking up at him, when Anthony opened his mouth to say something Amanda held up a finger and answered an emergency call.

"Michigan emergency this is Amanda, what is your emergency?" she said into the head phones she was wearing. Is your husband breathing mam? do you need an ambulance she inquired? Hold the line I'll connect you with the fire department. Amanda tried to stall on the phone, Charlotte had always told her a day like this would come, and she wish she was as smart as her and knew what to do next. She had to lie and tell Anthony she had to meet with the Sargent to discuss one of her calls so she said she would call him later.

Amanda left her station and took the elevator down to the lobby to wait for Gunnar. Do you want to walk Gunnar asked her it's just two blocks down. We haven't walked together in years Amanda told him. The March air was refreshing and they talked the entire way. After you Madam Gunnar said opening the door to the restaurant to let Amanda go in first. Amanda and Gunnar had a very playful lunch. They acted like they were on a date and played with one another's feet under the table.

Everyone in the restaurant thought they were boyfriend and girlfriend on their first date. And later that night their love making was better than the night before and the next morning when Amanda woke a note was on Gunnar's pillow telling her he went for a run and he would be back in an hour. She laid there thinking how things had changed for them and thought she should call Charlotte and tell her the good news. She must have drifted back off to sleep dreaming about the day Charlotte came to live with her and her parents in New York when she was a freshmen in high school.

Jonnies sister Susan left the hospital very distraught after hearing she had cancer. She waited until Charlotte came home from school and gave her the bad news. When Charlotte entered the house her mom was sitting at the kitchen table with no lights on. Are you ok Charlotte asked her mom? I went to the doctor today and they say I have cancer, Susan told her fourteen year old daughter. They both hugged each other and cried for an hour in the kitchen.

Have you told anyone yet Charlotte asked her mom? No I wanted you to be the first to know her mom told her. I think you should call your sister Jonnie and let her know Charlotte said. I'll call her in the morning her mom said but first we need to talk. I'm going to be seeing a lot of doctors and I think you should move to New York and stay with Jonnie and her family until I'm all well. But who will take care of you when I'm gone Charlotte denounced? I will be in good hands her mom told her all the best doctors and medicines are right here in Michigan. I don't want to go but I'll do whatever you think is best. Charlotte slept with her mom that night and the next morning her mom called her sister in New York and gave her the news. Jonnie cried and told her sister she thought it was a good idea for Charlotte to come.

Frank and Jonnie Collins welcomed Charlotte into their home. Charlotte and Amanda were both fourteen and in the ninth grade. After three years Charlotte loved living with her aunt, uncle and cousin. She had only been back to visit her mom twice in the three years over summer break. Amanda loved having her there it was like the sister she never had. One morning as Jonnie was fixing breakfast for the family Charlotte came down stairs and said she wasn't feeling well. Frank felt her fore head and said she was burning up. I'll stay home and take you to the doctor Jonnie said.

Frank volunteered to drive Amanda to school and Jonnie told Charlotte to go up and get dressed. When Frank and Charlotte left Jonnie cleared the breakfast dishes and went up to get dressed. After she dressed she went to check on Charlotte. She walked into her nieces' room and heard the shower running. Jonnie looked around the room and on the book shelf was a set of encyclopedia's, Jonnie just pulled one out form the middle and sat in the bean bag in the corner of the room. When she was comfortable in the bean bag she opened the book and three pictures fell out onto the carpet.

Jonnie picked them up and when she looked at them she was shocked to see Charlotte and their next door neighbor Pete in an awkward position with smiles on their faces. The pictures disguised Jonnie so much she gathered the pictures up and put them back in the book and put the book back in its place on the book shelf and left the room while Charlotte was still in the shower. When Charlotte came down stairs Jonnie was sitting at the kitchen table having her third cup of coffee. Ok I'm ready Aunt Jonnie Charlotte said. They left out the kitchen door into the garage.

When they called Charlotte's name at the doctor's office she asked her aunt if she could go in alone, but Jonnie told her she was coming with her. Sometimes my mom let me go in by myself Charlotte cried not this time Jonnie told her doubting her every word and making a mental note to call her sister later and ask her. After they left the doctor's office Charlotte asked Jonnie if they could stop at McDonald's for burgers. I'm starving she told her aunt, oh I forgot you didn't eat breakfast, just let me get your prescription filled first and then we can stop.

When they returned home Charlotte said her head still hurt and she was going back to bed. When Jonnie checked on Charlotte at 2'oclock she was still sleeping so she decided to go meet Amanda at her bus stop. Mom what's wrong Amanda asked when she saw her mom waiting at her bus stop is Charlotte ok. Yes, just a bad headache her mom told her. Why are you here? Amanda asked her you haven't met me at my bus stop since I was twelve. I just wanted to talk to you before you made it home her mom told her. I just have one question and I want an honest answer from you even if you think it will hurt me I still want you to tell me the truth ok?

Ok mom you're scaring me is Aunt Susan ok? Yes she's finishing up her treatments and she says she has her appetite back. So what's up mom? Are you sexually active her mom asked her? "No" are you kidding me, that's gross mom. Amanda had already forgotten about the one time two years ago when she did it with Vincent Richardson and it hurt so bad she said she would never do it again and she hadn't.

What brought that on Amanda asked her mom? Do you know if Charlotte is sexually active Jonnie asked her? Mom you know I can't tell you that Amanda answered. So that means yes Jonnie said, don't worry I won't say anything. Amanda was quiet the rest of the walk home not looking at her mom thinking if she look her way she might think of something else to ask her.

Amanda helped her mom fix dinner that night and after dinner Charlotte said she felt much better and wanted to go to school tomorrow. The next morning when she came down Frank felt her fore head again and told her that it felt much better that morning. Maybe you don't eat enough he told her, but Charlotte was always thin and always concerned about her weight she never wanted to weight more than her one hundred and thirty pounds. Last year when she went to New York to visit her mom they went out to eat every day and she gained five pounds and when she got back to Michigan she starved herself until she lost the five pounds.

Jonnie took the next day off work, she wanted to tell someone about her niece and her neighbor Pete but she didn't know who to tell. After everyone left the house she went to look at the pictures again. This time she got a good look at them and noticed the brown and tan curtains in the back ground and the white teddy bear on the night stand that Frank had given her for valentine's day and then she noticed her headboard, "they were in my room she shouted out loud." Jonnie went back to her room looking for cameras. She knew that Tony at work knew about surveillance cameras so she called him and asked him if he could come by on his lunch break.

Sure what's up Tony asked, I need you opinion on something Jonnie told him. When Tony arrived at eleven thirty Jonnie asked him to search the house for cameras. Tony did a quick search and told Jonnie that he couldn't find any hidden cameras. After Tony left Jonnie decided to take an hour nap. When she started to get up she heard the front door open and then she heard Charlotte laughing and then a male's voice. Just to let them know she was there she let out a big cough, and the next thing she heard was the front door open and close again and when she looked out her bedroom window she saw a teen age boy running down the street, then she heard footsteps in the hall. She jumped back in her bed and covered herself as her door opened so Charlotte couldn't see that she was fully dressed. Aunt Jonnie are you ok Charlotte whispered. Yes Jonnie said in a scratchy voice I think I'm catching something. Is it 2:00 already Jonnie asked still playing the game? No my head was hurting again so I skipped my last two classes and came home. I'm going to my room and lay down Charlotte told her aunt.

Amanda came home and told her mom Charlotte wasn't on the bus. She came home early because her head was hurting, mom told her. The next morning Jonnie decided to stay home and use another one of her sick days she knew after three you would have to bring in a doctor's note. After everyone left she laid in her bed just staring at the celling and she noticed a tiny black dot in the corner and another one in the light fixture on the celling. She went into the garage and got the ladder. She climbed up on the ladder to get a closer look and noticed the black dot was a wire and when she jerked on the wire she heard a crash in the other room. She went into Charlotte's room and found a small hole in the wall connected to a wire and a camera. She immediately went to the phone and called her sister and told her that she was sending Charlotte home to stay.

She told her sister Charlotte was having sex and she didn't want her to influence Amanda. I knew she was sexually active before she came to live with you Susan admitted, I thought if she moved there she would change. They go on Spring break in two weeks and I think she should move back to Michigan and live with you. "Ok," her sister Susan said, you've had her for three years and I am so grateful to you and Frank for all you've done.

After hanging up from her sister Jonnie called a carpenter and ask if he could come fix a small hole in the wall. The carpenter came right away and fixed the hole and removed the camera before the girls came home. As the carpenter pulled his small truck out the driveway Pete was pulling into his driveway next door and gave Jonnie a big smile and a wave. It took all Jonnies strength to return the smile and wave back. Jonnie wondered if should have told her sister Charlotte was spying on her and Frank but she thought her sister already had too much on her plate and decided not to.

Amanda cried when her mom told her that Charlotte was going home for their spring break. The girls had grown so close over the three years since Charlotte had lived with them. Why can't I go too Amanda cried? I think she should give her mom all her attention Jonnie told Amanda. But I want to see Aunt Susan too Amanda pouted. Honey the cancer came back and now she's taking radiation and I think you would just be in the way and I don't want to put extra work on her. "I'm not extra work," Amanda screamed. "I can help out it's only for a week". Jonnie didn't want to tell her daughter Charlotte wouldn't be coming back after Spring break she wanted to wait until Susan told Charlotte herself after she got there.

On the last day of school before spring break Charlotte skipped her last three classes and went off with some friends but got back to school in time to take the bus home and no one knew she was not at school but her teachers and the friends she was with. Where is your cousin did she come home on the bus with you Jonnie asked? Yes she stopped in the drive way to say something to Mr. Pete Amanda said. When Charlotte walked in the house Jonnie told her that her mom wants her to come home for Spring break again like last year. I already ordered your plane ticket and your plane leaves at seven.

Charlotte left the kitchen to pack her bag and Frank walked in from the garage. Can you take Charlotte to the airport after dinner Jonnie asked him? Sure, where's she going Frank asked, the same place she goes every year Jonnie snapped. Frank and Amanda gasped and asked her did something happen that we should know about? No just leave the kitchen dinner's in thirty minutes. What are we having Amanda asked, sloppy joes and fries Jonnie responded not looking at her daughter.

After dinner Charlotte went to get her bag and when she returned she told Amanda to stay out of her room while she's gone. I want it to stay just the way I left it. You won't have to clean in there she told her aunt, I just cleaned it up. OK dear Jonnie smile at her niece. You mean I don't get that office I always wanted

Frank teased. "No," Uncle Frank don't you dare put a desk in my room, I barley have enough room for all my stuff, which was the guest room that Charlotte had been using for the last 3 years was the biggest bed room in the house. It had 2 large windows when her and Franks master bed room had two small windows, and Amanda's bed room had only 1 window.

Charlotte and Amanda's bed room was separated by a bathroom which both girls shared that could only be entered through one of their rooms and not from the hall. Sometimes Amanda would take baths in her mom's tub in the master bath because it had jets in the tub. Two hours later Charlotte was on the plane from New York to Michigan.

The plane ride took less than two hours. Amanda rode with her dad to the airport and the girls cried in each other's arms at the gate. Now remember Frank told her this is the ticket you give to the lady at the gate and your gate number is B12 and when you get there just have a seat and wait for them to call your seat number which is 14A and when you board the plane put your bag under the seat in front of you or over your head. And then Frank gave her money for a cab from the airport to her mom's house.

Amanda waited at the gate waving at Charlotte each time she looked back. She was like a sister to her and she would miss her. They got along so well together telling each other's secrets. Charlotte even knew when Amanda did it with Vincent Richardson behind the bleachers at school for the first time. Amanda also knew Charlotte had did it before she even came to New York three years ago to live with them.  They were closer than sisters, more like twins because they looked so much alike. People at school thought they were sisters and they never told them any different. Charlotte hadn't seen her mom in a year because the cancer had come back and her mom had to start another treatment. Now she only had one more radiation to get and hopefully this would be the end of the cancer. Now she would really see her mom in the flesh not just on Skype on her computer, now she would actually be able to give her a real hug.

When Frank and Amanda returned from the airport the three of them played games until nine and Amanda got up and said she was going to her room to call Charlotte. Charlotte was glad to hear from her and told her that her mom wanted her to stay and she probably won't be coming back. Two months later Susan was cancer free and Charlotte didn't want to leave her again. The next year after Amanda graduated from high school she went to Michigan to live with her aunt Susan and cousin. Charlotte took her to parties every weekend and at one of the parties Amanda met Gunnar who was much older than her and he told her he had two sons ages one and two years old, Wow you don't waste no time Amanda smiled at him. They did it that night and the next month Amanda found out she was pregnant.

When Amanda woke again she heard voices down stairs and looked at the clock she was surprised to see it was ten fifty five. She got up and went into her bathroom to wash her face and brush her teeth. When she came out Gunnar was entering the room with a tray. Is that for me Amanda asked? Yes Gunnar said I thought you might be hungry. And I get flowers too Amanda smiled? You haven't brought me flowers in 10 over years.

Where are the girls Amanda asked? They are down stairs trying to make cookies if they ask you if you want any say you're not hungry because I'm not eating any. Why not Amanda laughed? Unless you like egg shells in your cookies I suggest you not eat any when they offer you some.

Ok thanks for the tip Amanda laugh. As soon as she said that Madison came rushing in the room with a plate full of cookies. Mommy look what we made, don't they smell delicious? Take one while they're hot. Oh honey your dad just fixed me this big breakfast and I don't know if I'll have room for cookies. Ok mommy we'll save you some Madison said and you too daddy. Is Aunt Charlotte coming over Madison asked? I'll save some for her too we made plenty.

When Madison left the room with the cookies they both laughed. Gunnar and Amanda spent the entire day with the girls doing nothing then at dinner he told them he had booked a four day cruise to the Bahamas and they would be leaving in three days. Will Major be going too Madison asked? "Yes," Gunnar said I'll call him after I finish dinner. It's going to be boring without Gun Kendra confessed he's the daring one.

After dinner Gunnar went to his study to call Major to break the news about the trip. "Wow that's cool dad I'm going to pack right now". The next day Amanda took the girls to the beauty shop and they all got their hair done and three days later they were on their way to the airport to Florida. Madison always wanted the window seat on the plane the rest of them didn't care. When they landed in Florida they took a shuttle to the ship.

Wow Madison said, it looks even bigger than last year. The line was a block long to get in but Gunnar and his family were platinum and they walked pass everyone else standing in line and went through the VIP door. Ten minutes later they were boarding the ship. They went straight to the Lido deck for lunch then after lunch they went on a tour of the ship. After the tour they went to the twelfth floor to see if their suite was ready. When they entered the suite all the beds were made and there was a bottle of Champaign chilling in the ice bucket  a dozen roses in a vase on the table and a cheese try with chocolate covered strawberries.

Why don't you kids go have fun until our bags arrive Gunnar told them me and your mom will stay here and relax out on the patio. After the kids left Gunnar took the champagne and two glasses out on the patio and they sat there and talked. You've been so tensed lately now you look more relax. I'm sorry Amanda said leaning back in her chair letting the sun hit her face. We lost two officers in a shootout. Yea I read that in the paper did you know them? No Amanda said but just the thought they're out there to help and then get shot in the process.

They heard the door open and house keeper was bringing their bags in. Would you like for me to unpack your bags the man asked? Yes please, Gunnar told him and the man left them to relax on the patio and went to unpack their bags. Gunnar told her he was under stress at the Social Security Administration Office also people think we're holding back on their money and think they should be getting more than what their getting and when I tell them I don't make the rules they say let me speak to your supervisor and when I send them to Mr. Johnson's office he looks at me like you can't do your job? I think I might be ready to retire again.

So that means we would have to cut down on our four cruises a year Amanda asked? Yes we'll still take the one for Spring break and in the summer, we may have to give up the one for Thanksgiving and Christmas. The kids came bouncing back into the room and out on the patio with them are our bags here yet Major asked? Yes your bags have been unpacked already Gunnar told him ok I'm going swimming he said going back inside me too Madison said following her brother I think I'll get in the whirlpool Kendra told them. That sounds nice Amanda said I think I'll join you. You have one at home that you never use Gunnar said. Ok you go and I'll take a short nap until we have to do the drill.

The rest of the cruse went great Gunnar was hoping Amanda wouldn't get depressed again when they returned home. On the plane ride back to Michigan everyone was in good spirits.  The next week everything went back to normal the kids went back to school and Amanda and Anthony continued their afternoon ritual every day unless there was an emergency and Anthony had to rush out. Gunnar went back still thinking about retiring. Eight weeks later Madison came home with her cap and gown for graduation which was the following Friday and Kendra came home with her grades and a big smile on her face. I passed my classes with all A's I can't wait to be a junior next year. Hey we will be at the same school Madison said.

Jonnie and Frank arrived two days before Madison's graduation and booked a room at the Marriott. You could have stayed here Amanda told her parents when they called and told her they had arrived. Oh this is just fine Jonnie claimed.  Ok I have you and dad's tickets and we would have to meet up before the graduation to get your tickets. Is that grandma Madison asked coming into the kitchen? Yes it is grandma Amanda told Madison I want to talk she said taking the phone from her mom before waiting for a response hi grandma, Madison said are you on the way? We are here at our hotel Jonnie  told Madison  I thought you and grandpa was staying here, not this time Jonnie told her well I'm going to get mom to bring me to your hotel which one are you at Madison asked?

We're at the Marriott but we were on our way out to your aunt Susan why don't we stop by there on our way back to the hotel? Okay Madison said and gave the phone back to her mom. Jonnie told Amanda they would stop by after they visit Susan. Should I fix dinner Amanda asked? No don't bother we will probably take Susan out to dinner. Amanda saw that Madison was upset when she hung up the phone and asked her did she want to go to the beauty shop and get her hair done while her grandma visit her sister?

After they left Gloria's on their way back to the hotel Jonnie told Frank that she wanted to stop at Amanda's. I'm not stopping Frank announced you can drop me off and take the rental car back to visit them I just don't like that man Frank told his wife. It's okay I'll call Madison and tell her we'll just see her tomorrow. Madison was not happy when her grandma called and said they were not coming.

At the graduation the next day Amanda and Jonnie cried when Madison's name was called to walk across the stage and receive her diploma. After the graduation everyone went out to Madison's favorite restaurant. Gunnar complemented Jonnie on her dress and Frank did his best to be civil towards him. Gunnar told Gloria how nice it was to see her again and she looked well. I'm doing much better Gloria told him Charlotte has been a big help in my recovery she told them. Oh Mom that's so Sweet Charlotte answered but I can't take the credit for that you are a good trooper. How long are you staying Kendra asked? We will be leaving tomorrow Jonnie told them.

Why so soon Amanda asked we never get to see you. I am coming for the summer Madison told them. I have to go to my brother's graduation in two days then I will come to New York. That's fine dear her grandma told her. Frank and Jonnie left the next day and two weeks later Madison was on a plane to New York for the summer. Kendra spent the summer seeing Kevin every day doing fun activities. This would be the first summer we haven't been on a cruise in over 10 years Gunnar told Amanda. The next day Amanda and Charlotte met for lunch and Amanda told her cousin she couldn't stop thinking about Vincent Roberson. You just need to wipe that man out of your head and forget he ever existed or you're going to go crazy. But what if they get married one day Amanda cried? They won't Charlotte declare no one marries their first love.

Jalaya Jaleese Moore shared a dorm room with two other girls, Valencia and Yolanda. Valencia's parents came at one forty five and took her home. Valencia's parents were an odd couple, her dad was 5.5 and her mom was 5.9 and they called each other Mr. and Mrs. Easterland and Valencia called them both by their first name. They made two trips down to their van with Valencia's things. The last bag sat by the door and Valencia's mom turned to her dad and said ok Mr. Easterland get the last bag and we'll wait in the van while she says her goodbyes to her friends.

Mr. Easterland struggled with the last bag while Mrs. Easterland held the open door for him. The three girls hugged and Valencia said she would call when she got home. Yes you make sure you do that Yolanda said. What time are your parents coming she asked them? Mine should be on the way Jalaya said. My parents will be here some time tonight or in the morning Yolanda said. I can't wait to get home to see how big my cat has gotten Valencia said laughing. I sure miss that fur ball. We know Yolanda and Jalaya said in unison, you keep her picture next to your bed. I can't help it Amber sat in the palm of my hand when I first got her and I fell in love with her orange hair. Well I have to go, you girls be good and I'll call when I get home Valencia told them giving them one last hug, I'll see you in September. When Valencia got in the van she sat in the front seat with her mom who was driving and her dad sat in the second row of seats with all Valencia's things.

After Valencia left Yolanda and Jalaya looked at one another. It's going to be strange being away from here for three months Yolanda sighed. What's stranger is that we will be sophomores when we come back. I'm glad we all picked to be in some of the same classes next year Jalaya told her. Well do you have all your stuff ready Mrs. Easterland Yolanda asked? Yes Mr. Easterland I do Jayala laughed trying to mimic Mr. Easterland. Both girls fell back in their beds laughing. I like them Jalaya said they're odd but they're cute. And speaking of cute I think your dad is hot Yolanda said. Well I'm going to have to agree with you on that

Jalaya laughed, he is hot. I think I got my looks from him Jalaya said turning sideways showing Yolanda her profile. No I can't see it Yolanda said laughing and Jalaya threw a pillow at her.

Anthony and his wife didn't say a word the first thirty minutes as he drove to JJ's college to bring her home for summer break. As he drove he was hoping she hadn't found out about Amanda, women had a way of sensing things like that even though nothing never seriously happened between them or maybe she's just quiet because she's tired Anthony thought? He decided to break the silence in the car. Are you ok Anthony asked Tiffany reaching across the car seat to touch her hand? No I have a lot on my mind was Tiffany's response. "oh no" here it comes Anthony thought. I was going to wait until we picked up J to tell you both together. "Oh no" she knows Anthony thought.

Sweat started popping out on his fore head even with the air conditioner on in the car. Maybe you should tell me first Anthony said. Maybe we can solve it without getting J involved. What are you talking about his wife looked at him confused? What are you talking about Anthony shot the question right back? I'm pregnant Tiffany announced with her head down. You're what? Anthony declared making the car swirl a little. Are you sure? Yes I went to the doctor this morning and it's confirmed. You seem sad Tiffany muttered. No just shocked I wasn't expecting that Anthony sighed. That's something you don't tell a person while they're driving, especially to pick up their eighteen year old daughter from college.

Well are you happy Tiffany asked him? I'm elated Anthony told her thinking now he would have to end it with Amanda. It was a shock to me too his wife was saying. I thought I had the flu she reached in her purse and pulled out a cigarette but Anthony took it from her hand before she got it to her mouth. You could say goodbye to these he told her and crumbled the cigarette up and threw it out the car window. We won't tell J in front of her friends, we'll wait until we're on the way back in the car Tiffany said. Then they got quiet again both in their own thoughts. After an hour Tiffany asked are you sure you're ok with this? Anthony took her hand and said you have made me one happy man and I can't wait to have laughter in our home again then he put her hand to his lips and kissed it. She leaned over and gave him a kiss on his right cheek.

Ok papa it won't be all laughter or have you forgot how it works? For the next seventeen years there will be laughter, crying, and lack of sleep, poopy diapers, and car pool and soccer games. Oh yes I forgot all that Anthony laughed. Can't we just skip that part? It doesn't work that way dear his wife said. Ok I'll take it all except for the diaper part Anthony said. Oh no buddy it doesn't work that way, you take one you take all, they both laughed.

They arrived at the University Of Illinois at 7:00 pm five hours after Valencia's parents had picked her up.

When they entered JJ's dorm building girls were running around rushing here and there. Dads were coming down the stairs with big suit cases. Some girls were hugging each other crying, mothers were bellowing out orders, phones were ringing in the distance the whole place seem like a war zone.

Anthony and Tiffany climbed the stairs to the second floor and on the way up they passed a dad struggling with three suit cases and a sock was hanging out of one of the suit cases. On their way down the hall to their daughter's room they passed the ringing phone that no one bothered to answer. When they reached their daughters room and knocked Jalaya opened the door to her parents smiling and holding hands. She looked at them puzzled and said who are you and what did you do with my parents? She had never saw that side of them before. They were always so serious and business like even to each other but she liked the transformation and hoped it last the next three months while she was home.

On the ride home Jalaya showed her parents her finial grades. She held a 4.0 grade level for her entire freshman year at the University Of Illinois. Her parents were so proud of her and she always did her best to please them because she knew how much they both wanted her to succeed. Wow this is great her mom told her, you always make us so happy. Yes I always wanted a little sister or brother to compare myself with but you guys had me and put the cork in it. They both laughed at her illustration. Well the cork is out now her dad laughed. What are you talking about Jalaya asked? You know that little sister or brother you always wanted? Well they will be here in nine months. Are you kidding me Jalaya asked shocked? Aren't you too old to still be having babies? That's what I thought her mom said but my body says different.

A week after Jalaya was home she needed something to keep her busy so she decided to go get her hair and nails done, while sitting under the dryer she noticed the sign on the wall asking for a shampoo girl. While she was in the chair getting her hair styled she inquired about it and was told she would have to put in an application. On Jalays way out she filled out the application and left it at the front desk. Two days later the beauty shop called her and asked when she can start. Right now Jalaya jumped for joy. Well come on in the owner told her we are backed up. Jalaya took the bus to the shop and was given a plastic apron and lead to the shampoo station. When she left five hours later she had washed twenty five heads. Her hours were twelve to four Tuesday, Wednesday, Friday and Saturday. She bragged to her parents that she was making her own money. That's sweet they told her let's see how much of it you can save Anthony told her.

Who wants burgers on the grill Gunnar Sr. called up the stairs? That sounds good Amanda said from the top of the stairs. She went to her daughters room knocked once and opened the door. Dad is putting burgers on the grill Amanda told her. Kendra was laying across her bed talking to Kevin. Can I invite Kevin Kendra asked covering the phone with her hand. Sure Amanda told her, how will he get here? I'll see if his dad could bring him Kendra said. When Vincent dropped Kevin off Amanda made sure she was upstairs in her room. She watched out of her bedroom window as he dropped Kevin off and drove away.

They ate burgers and grilled vegetables and after they were finished they played cards. I should call my dad to come get me now Kevin said. No I'll take you home Gunnar told him. I'm going too Kendra replied. You may as we'll come for the ride Gunnar told Amanda. After they dropped Kevin off Gunnar said he wanted to stop and check on Gunnar Jr. and Dominique.

Gunnar Jr. and Dominique did nothing but sit around all day doing nothing ever since Gunnar Jr. graduated from high school. Shouldn't you two be out doing something Patricia Clark asked one day, don't you have doctor appointments or something? Yes when do you go to the doctor Gunnar Jr. asked? Everything is fine Dominique complained and stormed out. Is she taking her medicine every day Patricia asked Gunnar Jr.? I never see her take any medicine he told her. Patricia went to her daughter's room and walked in without knocking and Dominique was pulling a shirt over her head and her mom noticed her flat stomach. Mom get out of my room, can't you knock Dominique yelled?

How many months did you say you were Patricia asked? I'm five months Dominique argued. No you're not her mom said closing the door so Gunnar wouldn't hear them talking. What have you done Dom? Her mom asked. Dominique covered her face with her hands and cried. Patricia went to her daughter and embraced her. I love him so much mom, he's the only boy that ever paid me any attention and I couldn't lose him you understand don't you mom? Dominique cried. You have to fix this Patricia told her. It's too late Dominique cried harder. No it's not, you need to fix this and you need to fix it now Patricia told her. They won't understand Dominique told her. What are you going to do when they see you and don't see a stomach Patricia asked?

Your husband in there don't seem to have a clue how this works. But his parents will find out soon enough because they think they will be grandparents in four months. Patricia heard Gunnar talking to someone in the other room and asked Dominique to be quiet for a minute. The next voice they heard was Kendra telling her brother she missed him. What are they doing here Dominique asked? Well here's your chance Patricia told her. I'm scared mom, I rather die. Don't you dare say that, what are they gonna do? They can't hurt you, I won't let them. Can you tell them Dominique asked? Oh no you started it now end it so you can go on with your life and stop living this lie. Patricia guided Dominique out and to the living room where Gunnar was talking to his parents and sister.

When Amanda looked up and saw Dominique she gasped. Go on Patricia urged her daughter. I'm sorry, did you lose the baby Kendra cried? No I was never pregnant. What? Wait, what are you saying Gunnar Jr. screamed? I'm sorry I didn't want to lose you so I lied Dominique explained. So you let him think you were pregnant when you knew he had a scholarship to attend college in Maryland Amanda fretted. Now just wait Patricia blew up who do you think your talking to? I'll tell you what, you better get all you can from this man because he will never marry you.  You have no right to talk to her that way Gunnar demanded. This is my home mister and you can't talk to me like that. You were behind this whole thing Gunnar yelled at Patricia.

Call the police Patricia told Dominique. No need Dominique we're leaving Gunnar Sr. Interjected. Are you coming son Gunnar Sr. asked? He's not staying here Patricia argued. Get your ass out of my house. Gunnar Jr. Looked at Dominique with tears in his eyes and asked why? You didn't have to take it this far. Come on son Gunnar Sr. sighed, let's go home. You will get annulment papers in the mail and I suggest you sign them. Gladly Patricia answered, just leave. And don't forget what I told you Patricia yelled to Amanda as they closed the door. I'll take you home and you explain to your mom what happened Gunnar Sr. told his son, then get all your college papers together you will be leaving in two months.

I'm sorry dad Gunnar Jr. breathed. Its ok Amanda spoke up, you didn't know. Thank you for being on my side he told her. I have always been on your side Amanda smiled at him in the back seat and Kendra took his hand and told him they all love him. All this time I had the best family anyone could ever ask for and didn't know it. When they dropped Gunnar Jr. off Gunnar drove off before his son knocked because he couldn't deal with Traci right now. What just happened Kendra asked?

The next day Amanda was off and decided to go get her hair done. You must be new she said to the girl shampooing her hair. I've been here a week Jalaya told her. Yes that feels good Amanda told her closing her eyes and enjoying the shampoo. Deep condition Jalaya asked? Yes Amanda said. When Amanda returned home she heard Gunnar in his den talking on the phone with the door closed, she heard the anger in his voice and headed to the kitchen to start lunch. He only had two more days off on his vacation before he return to work and she think he would be happier if he was at work then he wouldn't have to deal with all the drama going on at home. He never commented to her on what Patricia Clark said to her yesterday so she just thought she would leave it alone like she always do.

The next day she met Anthony at the cafe and he gave her good news that Isadore was back at work. So soon Amanda asked? He said he's fine Anthony told her. Well I'm glad he recovered, yea me too Anthony said.

Anthony's radio went off and he told Amanda he had to run. Ok be safe Amanda told him and gave him a kiss. For the next two weeks they met every day and ate lunch together. Tiffany told her boss she would work until the doctor tell her to stop then she wouldn't be back.

Amanda went to the beauty shop on her day off to get her hair done the following week. Jalaya was there and washed her hair again. You have magic hands she told Jalaya. Thank you I'm glad you enjoy it mam. Please call me Amanda, ok Amanda, I'm Jalaya it's nice to meet you Jalaya Amanda smiled. When Amanda got home Kendra was not there so she decided to call Charlotte. I can't talk right now Charlotte told her, I'm showing a house. You're doing good Amanda told her, this is the second one this week. I know Charlotte laughed I'll call you later.

Amanda decided to start dinner. She sat in front of the TV snapping string beans when Charlotte called her back and told her they liked the house and she think they're going to buy it. Amanda told her everything that's been going on there and asked Charlotte did she want to come over for lunch. I told mom I would be home for lunch Charlotte told her but you can meet me at my house and eat with us. No thanks Amanda said, I'll pass I'll just make me a salad. You sure Charlotte asked? Mom always make too much. I'm sure Amanda said give her a kiss for me. Amanda sat there watching TV snapping the string beans and found herself missing her parents, something she hadn't done in a long time. She wondered what Madison was up to.

That evening over dinner she asked Kendra did she want to fly to New York with her on Friday for the weekend. What I'm not invited Gunnar joked? I don't think you would enjoy yourself staying at my parents Amanda laughed. Just kidding Gunnar said, you girls go and have a nice time and kiss my little princess for me, who? My grandma Kendra asked? They all laughed. Thursday was Amanda's last day before she was off for the weekend. She told Anthony her plans and he told her to have fun in New York and to bring him a souvenir back. He told her his daughter JJ was home for the summer and he wanted to spend some time with her before she went back.

When Amanda got off Wednesday she decided to stop at the mall and pick up a couple of shorts outfits to take to Madison. While walking in Ross Clothing Store she saw Jalaya looking at baby clothes. Amanda walked up beside her and said is there something I should know? Oh hey Amanda Jalaya said, no, my mom is pregnant and this is for my baby brother or sister. Awe that's so sweet Amanda smiled. Do you like it Jalaya asked? Yes Amanda told her but this one is cuter Amanda said picking up the yellow sweater with matching booties. How much is that one Jalaya asked? Fifteen dollars Amanda said and seen the look in Jalayas face.

Hey why don't I give you half on it and that way I can say I gave something to the baby also Amanda said?

You would do that Jalaya asked? Are you hungry
Amanda asked? I don't know if I have enough Jalaya
told her, I don't like to ask my parents for money I like
to make my own. You are the ideal child Amanda told
her. Come on let's pay for your purchase and go get
something to eats. Over Japanese food in the food
court Amanda and Jalaya made small talk. Amanda
asked her how she liked working at the beauty shop
and Jalaya told her she loved it because she gets to
meet new friends. Amanda told her she has two
daughters in high school and her oldest daughter has
a boyfriend. I don't know about a boyfriend right now
Jalaya told her, I don't think I'm ready. What if she
gets pregnant?

Well she says they're not sexually active Amanda said.
Well you just keep an eye on her Jalaya told Amanda
because it can go further without them even planning
it. Then they heard a loud thunder, oh I better go
Jalaya said, I'm on the bus I'll take you home Amanda
told her. Where do you live? Jalaya gave Amanda her
address and Amanda told her wow that's a nice area.
On the way out the mall they passed a photo booth
and Jalaya looked at Amanda and laughed, let's do it
she laughed.

They took four pictures posing differently on each.
When the pictures came out they laughed at their
expressions. Do you have any scissors Jalaya asked?
Oh no you're not sticking them with me Amanda
laughed. Jalaya stuck the picture in her backpack. The
rain was coming down lightly when they exited the

mall. They ran to Amanda's car and when they got in they were both laughing like two old friends.

When Amanda started the car Jalaya was surprised to hear that Amanda liked listening to the latest music. I like that song Jalaya sang alone with the radio. You have a nice voice Amanda told her. Thanks, I got it from my grandmother Jalaya told her because my mom and dad can't hold a note even if they tried, this made Amanda laugh. Your parents must be so proud of you Amanda told her, you must be the oldest, wait you missed your turn Jalaya interrupted her. Take the next right and circle back. Amanda stopped talking and concentrated on the road. Now make the next right Jalaya told her, now make a left at the end of this block she told Amanda.

Amanda said I will have to use my GPS to get back home. No it's just because you missed that first right its easy just make a right and a left and that will put you back on the main street. Ok thanks Amanda told her, Jalaya was easy to talk to and she always made Amanda laugh even while she shampooed her hair. Amanda told her she was leaving tomorrow for New York to see her parents and she would see her at the shop when she returned. Ok Jalaya told her getting out the car, have a nice time in New York. Thanks Amanda responded now remember a right and a left, ok thanks Amanda said and drove off.

The next day Gunnar dropped them off at the airport and told them he would pick them up Sunday evening. "Bye daddy", Kendra told her dad and gave him a kiss on his cheek and Amanda gave him a soft kiss on the lips and he gave her a pat on her back side and a wink. You girls hurry back he told them. On the plane Amanda gave Kendra the window seat and she read her emails on her tablet until the announcement came on to turn off all electronic devices until the plane reaches a reasonable climate and they would let you know when you can turn them back on.

Kendra took one last picture out the window before turning off her phone. When the plane reached thirty five thousand Amanda turned her tablet back on while Kendra put her head phones on to hear the movie that was playing on the screen. When the stewardess came around Amanda ordered coffee and Kendra ordered coke. Amanda turned her tablet off to drink her coffee then leaned her head back and closed her eyes.

The next thing she heard was ladies and gentlemen please fasten your seat belts and put your seats in an upright position and prepare for landing, the stewardess will be coming around one last time to pick up all your empty containers and please turn off all electronic devices until the plane has landed. Kendra looked out the window and told her mom to look. New York was coming into view. It's beautiful here she told her mom. Why did you ever leave? I wanted to be close to Charlotte Amanda told her. You left all your friends to be with your cousin Kendra asked puzzled? We were and still are very close Amanda told her. But you had graduated didn't you

have a boyfriend? No, not until I met your dad
Amanda told her.

Frank was waiting for them when they exit the plane.
Kendra ran to her grandfather and gave him a big hug,
hi grandpa are you alone? Yes Madison and your
grandmother is making a big surprise for you all at
home. Hi dad, Amanda walked up and gave her dad a
kiss. Did you check any bags Frank asked? Nope this
is it Amanda told him. On the drive home Amanda
asked about Madison. She has been a joy to your
mom, she's in your old room and your mom goes in
and kisses her goodnight every night. She also helped
your mom plant a garden out back. Do you remember
our neighbor Pete? Yes Amanda said. Well he and his
wife separated and they're selling the house. Oh that's
too bad Amanda said. Yes I know Frank said I really
liked them and Pete and I were talking about starting
a bowling team.

Where are they moving to Amanda asked? Pete is
staying in New York but I think his wife is moving
back home to North Carolina. How could anyone
move from New York? Kendra asked with her nose
pressed against the car window, it's beautiful here.
Yes it is Frank said but very expensive. I never knew
that coming up Amanda said I always thought we had
lots of money and was well off. We were comfortable
Frank laughed but a long way from rich.

They pulled into the drive way and a big banner was
draped across the porch reading "WELCOME
AMANDA and KENDRA" awe that's nice Kendra said.

Jonnie and Madison came rushing out to the car to greet them. Hi Grandma, Kendra said giving her a big hug then she hugged her sister. How are you Jonnie asked Amanda? I'm good mom, happy to be home for a couple of days, when you left after Madison's graduation I found myself missing you guys. I miss you mommy Madison said giving her mom a big hug. We'll come on in Jonnie said we made cookies. Not my favorite Amanda squalled? Yep oatmeal raisins Madison said with a big smile on her face. How am I supposed to lose weight eating homemade oatmeal raisin cookies Amanda told them? I think you look nice just the way you are Frank said looking at his daughter with a questioning eye thinking if Gunnar had told her she was gaining too much weight.

Oh thank you daddy Amanda said kissing her dad, but you have to say that, I'm your daughter. The aroma hit their noses when they walked into the house and there were three balloons in the front room floating in the air. Oh you guys are too much Amanda said. I should come home more often being greeted like this. In the kitchen Madison and Jonnie had prepared finger sandwiches, a fruit and vegetable tray with dip, fresh lemonade and of course the cookies. Mommy I'm sleeping in your old bed Madison told her mom. It's very comfortable with a new mattress and four pillows. You two can sleep in the larger room Madison offered.

We'll thank you Amanda laughed. Grandpa has his desk in there but it won't be in your way Madison added. Everyone at the table laughed at Madison's serious expression. That was delicious Amanda said after they finished eating their lunch. I think I gained about three pounds. Frank looked at his daughter and then he knew for a fact that Gunnar must have been pressuring her about her weight. After lunch Amanda showed Madison the new clothes she bought her from the mall. Thank you mom I love them Madison crowed. For the rest of the day they sat around laughing and talking until Frank told them he was going out and would be back shortly. Is he ok Amanda asked her mom after her dad left?

Yes he's retiring next month and I think he's just a little antsy about that. Mom I found a checker board and checkers in your room Madison said, grandma said you, grandpa and Charlotte use to play checkers all the time. Oh wow I remember Amanda smiled thinking about how her dad would always let her win. I haven't played checkers since I left home. Do you want to play now Madison asked her mom? Grandpa taught me how to play. Sure I'll play Amanda told her. When Madison and Amanda went upstairs Jonnie asked Kendra about her boyfriend. His name is Kevin Richardson Kendra told her grandma and his mom is from Florida but I don't know where his dad is from. He has older twin sisters that are two years older than him.

So is this serious Jonnie asked her? If you're asking me about sex Kendra said I'm not ready for that yet. That's a good girl Jonnie said and gave her granddaughter a hug. Then they heard squalls from upstairs. Well someone is winning up there Jonnie laughed. When Frank returned they were all upstairs and came down when they heard him come in. Where did you go Jonnie asked? To get this Frank said and showed them the tickets to a famous play starting tomorrow.

Wow I heard about this play Amanda said. I was waiting for it to come to Michigan. Well now you don't have to Frank told her. You girls have third row seats tomorrow at the three O' clock show. Thank you they all told Frank with lots of hugs and kisses. Can we have hotdogs on the grill Madison asked? Grandpa makes the best grilled hotdogs Madison told her sister. It's all in the wrist Frank laughed. I'll make the salad Madison offered. They all sat around eating, laughing and enjoying their dinner. After dinner they all played checkers and Frank let them all win one game. At ten thirty Friday night they all decided to go to bed.

Amanda called Gunnar when she got in the bed and told him about the play. I thought we were going to wait until it came to Michigan and go together he asked? Dad just came home and surprised us with them she told him then made a fake yarn telling him she was going to sleep now. Did you even take clothes to wear to a play he asked? No Amanda told him, I'll wear one of mom's dresses and I will have to buy the girls a dress tomorrow. Ok enjoy the play and goodnight Gunnar told her. She loved Gunnar but she didn't want to hear him talking bad about her father.

The next morning Frank had breakfast on the table when the girls came down. Thanks dad Amanda smiled at the beautiful table her dad had set, you're going to spoil me. I know you do all the cooking in your house I just wanted to give you a break Frank said. Does he help you out at all Frank questioned? "Dad stop. "His name is Gunnar and I'm sure if I needed help in the kitchen that he would help me". I'm just asking a question Frank said. No you're not. I know what you're doing Amanda told him. How would you like your eggs Frank asked? Over easy is fine, Amanda said.

After breakfast all the girls went down town shopping. I miss this Amanda said looking up at all the tall buildings. We don't have this in Michigan. They stopped in Sak's 5th Ave, and Amanda was able to go off by herself and find an elegant gold pen and pencil set for Anthony. Then they went to Bloomingdales and they finally found the girl's dresses at Neiman Marcus then headed back home. Frank was out back tending to the garden when they returned. Will you be dropping us off Jonnie asked him? Yes Frank told her, I will chauffeur my favorite girls tonight. That's what my daddy calls us Madison laughed.

After a light lunch of fresh salad with cut up chicken and garlic bread the girls went up to get ready. Madison put her hair up into a pony tail leaving bangs in the front and asked her sister to curl her pony tail with the curling irons. At 2:00 they were all dressed and ready to go. When they came down Frank's eyes watered and told them they look like black angles. Frank pulled the car out and opened the doors for them. All of you look so beautiful he told them again on the drive downtown. Jonnie wore a dress she had purchased two months earlier. Cream color with pearl buttons down the front with a low back. She wore black strap saddles with no stockings and the diamond earrings Frank had given her for Mother's Day last year from Tiffany's.

Amanda wore Jonnies light green two piece dress set. The dress was sleeveless and had tinny pleats on the hem and a cute little matching jacket with one button in the front. She wore her mom's jewelry to match her outfit. Kendra's dress was short and cute. It had two tones of purple, a high collar and three quarter inch sleeves. She wore saddles to show off her new ankle bracelet and borrowed jewelry from her grandma's jewelry box. Madison wore a nude color designer three quarter length dress with lots of sequence with a sweetheart neck line and hand beaded pearls and rhyme stones. She also wore elegant sandals with one half inch hills.  Frank pulled in front of all the cars lined up at The Music Box Theater on forty Fifth Street and opened the doors to let the girls out. I'll be waiting out here when you come out he told them. When they entered the Theater they felt like Cinderella going to the ball.

The play the music the scenery the actors everything was superb. During half time the girls had to stand in line for the ladies room. I can't wait to see if she dies Madison said while they waited in line, or if he finds her in time Kendra said. When they came out the ladies room the light on top of the doors were on indicating it was time to enter the theater and take their seats again. During the second half they heard sniffles in the crowed when the man found the girl and even more when the girl opened her eyes. When Madison looked at her grandmother she seen that her eyes were wet and when she looked at her sister her eyes were wet also. I can't move Kendra said after the play ended and when she looked around she wasn't the only one. People were still seated drying their eyes. What a superb play the lady seated behind them was saying. Excellent the other female with her said.

When they exit the theater it was hard to find Frank due to the big crowd. Kendra took her cell phone out and called him. He told them to just stay in front of the theater that he was in a long line of cars and would be there shortly. The cars and cabs were moving quickly, they saw Frank's car moving toward them. Some of the responses to the play they heard around them were phenomenal, effortless, mesmerizing, they danced with such sincerity, every move they made was true emotion there was no faking it, and I was blown away with the performance and amazing choreography.

When Frank finally reached them he got out and came to the other side to open the doors for them. On the ride home they told Frank about the play. I knew you would like it Frank said. Well you girls hungry? I'm still hyped from the play Kendra laughed. When they returned home the girls took off their gowns and put on shorts. Frank made kabobs on the grill and they all sat on the patio talking. What a perfect vacation Amanda sighed. I'm going to have to do this more often we would love that her mother said. That night they watched a good movie on TV and when the movie went off at eleven Amanda went up to set her hair in rollers and put her gown on, long gone were the comfortable pajamas she wore so long ago. She called Gunnar to tell him goodnight.

How was the play he asked? It was magnificent she told him. He told her he got Gunnar Jr. and Dominique marriage annulled and he will be going to Maryland in September to start his college freshman year. Wow you work pretty fast Mr. Bradley, Amanda laughed. Only when it come to my family I'm not going to let anyone play us for fools. I will be at the airport at eight twenty two tomorrow night when you girls get off the plane.

Will Mad be coming with you Gunnar asked? No she wants to stay a little longer Amanda told him. She's sleeping in my old room and enjoying it. Amanda told him how she found the old checker board in the closet now she thinks she's a pro. Oh no I better brush up on my game before she come home. Yes because she already said she's going to ask you to buy a checker game. Ok love you Gunnar told her and I'll see you tomorrow evening.

The next morning everyone slept in late except Jonnie. When they came down Jonnie was cleaning collard greens and had smoke ham hocks boiling on the stove. Umm what smells so good Amanda asked? I thought we would have a big dinner on your last day Jonnie smiled. Smothered fried chicken, macaroni and cheese and collard greens with them hush puppy cornbread you use to love and blackberry cobbler. I'm not going to be able to fit on the plane Amanda laughed. She made a mental note to herself to diet all next week to get the extra weight off from this weekend. She might have to skip a couple of her meals with Anthony.

What can I do Amanda asked her mom looking around the kitchen. You can cut the chicken up and wash it, yes mam Amanda laughed opening the refrigerator to get the chicken out. Amanda started cutting up chicken at the sink. Jonnie looked at her daughter worried. Is everything ok at home Jonnie inquired? Sure why do you ask Amanda asked? I don't know you look different than when I saw you a few weeks back. How different Amanda asked? I don't know more relaxed Jonnie said, like you had a lot on your mind. I'm always relaxed when I come home Amanda told her mom.

Then the kitchen got quiet again and Amanda was lost in her thoughts about how she was going to break it off with Kevin now that her and Gunnar was getting along better. Good morning Frank said as he entered the kitchen. Something smells delicious in here. I decided to start dinner early so we could sit down and eat with our daughter before she leaves. You can start breakfast if you want Jonnie told him. Just toast and coffee for me Frank said taking the coffee out the cabinet. Make that two Kendra said coming into the kitchen yawning in her bare feet.

When did you start drinking coffee Jonnie asked? Sometimes mom let me have a little of hers Kendra told her grandmother. When Madison finally came down everyone was sitting at the table drinking coffee and eating toast. Why do I smell greens this early in the morning Madison asked? And why is she drinking coffee Madison asked pointing to her sister? It's only a half cup Amanda laughed. I want some too Madison said with excitement in her voice. We have orange juice pored for you Jonnie said. When do I get to drink coffee Madison asked? She's only a year older than me.

After breakfast everyone left the kitchen except Jonnie and Amanda. This is like old times Jonnie said. Remember when you would come home from school and help me finish dinner? Yes I remember Amanda said. I liked snapping the fresh string beans just to hear the snap. But I didn't like potatoes. Do you still have that scar on your foot from the hot oil that peeling spilled when you were trying to fry chicken Jonnie asked? Yep it's still there Amanda said you wouldn't let me help you for two months Amanda laughed then when you did let me help again I almost cut my thumb off with the knife, I still have that scar too Amanda laughed that's when daddy told you not to let me help anymore.

They heard Frank, Kendra and Madison in the other room playing checkers. You can't move that one Madison was yelling at her sister. Grandpa tell her she can't move that one Madison pleaded. I'm going to lose it when you all leave Jonnie said, I just love the noise and laughter of children in the house. Is that so Amanda teased?

When I use to fuss at Charlotte for wearing my clothes without permission you would tell us we were too loud now you want noise in the house? You two were really going at it Jonnie said. I thought I was going to have to break up a fight the time she wore your new blouse without you knowing and spilled the milk on it at school. I hadn't even had a chance to wear it yet Amanda said. The way she kept that room I don't know how she could find anything in there. Yes she was a slob Amanda laughed, she's still that way now. When I go over to visit I always clean her bedroom for her. She kelp it closed when Frank and I was there Jonnie said. And we know why, they both laughed. Have you learned to make cornbread yet Jonnie asked? No I tried but mine just don't come out right Amanda told her. Its ok I'll make it and you can watch me.

Amanda and Jonnie talked softly in the kitchen while they cooked with the radio playing quietly in the back ground. They went out and got fresh vegetables out the garden and sat out in the back yard among the beautiful flowers that Frank tended to twice a day. It's been a long time since I just relaxed and did nothing Amanda said. It's always something going on in my house with two kids. When they came back in Madison was in the kitchen smiling. What's so funny Jonnie asked? We have a surprise for you, follow me. Amanda and Jonnie followed Madison into the dining room where Frank and Kendra was just finishing setting the table with Jonnies best china which she never got to use and had always hoped an occasion would come where she could use them.

Jonnie cried when she saw the beautiful tablet they had set with the china. I knew you would like it Frank said, I love it Jonnie cried I wish I would have thought of it. After the food was done Jonnie and Frank brought it to the table and they all sat down to eat. After they ate Frank said he couldn't eat another bite. But what about desert Amanda asked her dad? Well maybe I have a little room left they all laughed. After desert Kendra and Madison volunteered to clean up. After the kitchen was clean it was time for Amanda and Kendra to go to the airport. Madison and Jonnie rode with Frank to take them to the airport. Jonnie hugged her daughter and told her to come back soon. I will mom but you can't be cooking like that next time. Yes she can Kendra spoke up. You really should watch your weight Amanda told her daughter. Leave her alone she's just fine Frank spoke up.

At the airport they all said their goodbyes. When Gunnar picked them up from the airport he told them that Dominique was sent away to a psychiatric center for depression and was put on twenty four hour watch. That poor girl Amanda said. Poor girl? Don't feel sorry for her Gunnar shouted, she almost ruined our lives. When Amanda went to work Monday she and Anthony met for lunch at their place. Amanda gave him the gold pen and pencil set and he loved it giving her a kiss. They ate lunch together for the rest of the week and even thought things were going great at home with Gunnar, Amanda wasn't ready to give up what she had with Anthony yet.

On her day off she got up that morning and headed for the beauty shop. As she pulled into the lot she saw Jalaya getting out if a cream color Mercedes. And Amanda wondered who the petite, attractive, small framed women with the long ponytail and gorgeous chocolate skin as smooth as butter was dropping her off.

While Jalaya washed Amanda's hair she asked her about the women. Oh that's my mom Jalaya told her, I was running late this morning and my mom dropped me off. How is she Amanda asked? Oh she's fine and the baby is getting bigger. You sound like a proud big sister Amanda told her. I am Jalaya told her, and you should see my dad he's belated. He rubs her little belly every day talking to his son. That's funny Amanda laughed it's something about men and their sons. After Amanda got her hair blow dried and flat ironed she waved to Jalaya as she washed another patroness hair and told her she would see her in two weeks.

Two weeks later was the Fourth of July weekend and everyone was trying to get their hair done. Amanda was Jalays last patroness for the day and she was tired after standing on her feet washing hair all day so Amanda offered her a ride home. Thank you so much that would be nice Jalaya told her I was just going to call my dad. How's your mom feeling Amanda inquired? Oh they're so excited Jalaya laughed they act like two teenagers at home. That's nice Amanda smiled visualizing the couple smiling at each other the way her and Anthony smile at each other and the man rubbing his wife's belly.

When they reached Jalays home she wanted Amanda to come in and meet her parents. I would love to Amanda told her. When Amanda walked into Jalayas home she was amassed how beautiful it was. Everything in the house was neat and orderly and lavishly decorated in peach and cream color and the chandelier hanging over the front foyer was breath taking and Amanda found herself wondering how they cleaned it.

Come on Jalaya said taking Amanda's arm guiding her into another room. When they entered the room Amanda recognized Jalayas mom from when she dropped her off the day she was running late for the shop. Mom this is Mrs. Collins from the shop she gave me a ride home. That was so nice of you Mrs. Collins, Tiffany said standing please call me Amanda you don't have to stand Amanda told her. Your daughter is amazing I just love her to death. Yes she is amazing Tiffany agreed.

Well I must be going Amanda told them. Where's dad Jalaya asked? He's out back with uncle Mike Tiffany told her working on that old car again. I don't know why they spend so much money on that old thing Tiffany laughed. Well congratulations on the new baby Amanda told her. Thank you Tiffany told her I thought our baby days were over boy was I wrong, and he's a kicker I think he's playing football in there. They all laughed and Jalaya walked Amanda to the door. I'll see you in two weeks Amanda told her. Anthony and Amanda continue to have their lunch every day but Amanda noticed something different in Anthony.

Maybe he's just tired so she brushed it off. Two weeks later at the end of July Amanda is leaving the shop when she notice Jalaya saying goodbye to the owner. Take an umbrella the owner told her just in case it rains before you make it home. I can drop you off Amanda offered standing at the door. You are so sweet Jalaya told her but only if you take your tip back. I can't do that Amanda told her. What do you think I am, an Indian giver? Jalaya laughed, "Wow! I haven't heard that saying in a long time".

No I wouldn't want you to be an Indian giver whatever that is, both girls laughed. I would have to ask my dad about that Jalaya said he thinks he's pretty smart and know a little about everything. On the ride to Jalayas house Amanda asked about her mom again. She's fine thank you Jalaya said she went for her five month checkup and the baby is doing great. That's good news Amanda said. Oh and I have another surprise Jalaya smiled. It must be really big Amanda said according to that big smile on your face. It is, do you remember my mom telling you my dad and uncle has been working on a fourteen year old car giving it all new parts? Oh yes I think I remember Amanda said trying to remember, Uncle Mike wasn't it? Yes that's my dad's brother. Well any way they are almost finished and they are giving the car to me. Are you kidding me Amanda asked? No they told me yesterday. Your dad and uncle must really love you Amanda told her. Amanda pulled up to the house and told Jalaya she would see her in two weeks. No you have to come see the car Jalaya cried. Ok I would love to Amanda said turning the ignition off and getting out the car.

When Jalaya lead Amanda into her home Amanda observed Jalayas mom and dad snuggled in each other's arms and the man was smiling with his hand on his wife's protruding belly. Jalayas voice interrupted their private moment. Dad this is my friend Mrs. Collins. Tiffany smiled at Amanda and when her husband turned around to greet Amanda he froze, the smile left his face and his eyes got as big as saucers. Where are your manners Tiffany asked? Its nice meeting you Anthony said getting up and extending his hand to Amanda then fell over the ottoman. Oh are you ok daddy Jalaya said rushing to her dad helping him up. He took Amanda's hand and it was wet while his was ice cold he talked with his eyes never leaving hers their eyes stuck on each other's for about five seconds.

Amanda felt a jealous twinge stirring in her stomach down to her toes. She tilted her head in question then gyrated her head shaking away the memory. She told Jalaya she had to leave. But wait you haven't seen my car yet Jalaya squealed. Amanda moved swiftly to the front door and told her maybe next time. When Amanda left her mind was whirling with questions only Anthony could answer. When Amanda pulled into the garage she dried her wet eyes and checked the mirror before going inside. There was no one in the kitchen when she entered and she sat down at the table just to have a moment to herself. She heard the doorbell ring and jumped. Dad the pizzas here, Kendra called up stairs to her dad.

I'll get it Amanda told her walking into the living room. She pulled out her credit card and gave it to the pizza delivery man. He swiped her card on his portable machine and Gunnar appeared at the bottom of the stairs as Amanda was signing for the card. He gave the pizza man a generous tip and thanked him closing the door behind him. Kendra had already took the pizza into the kitchen. Is that a new hair style Gunnar asked? Yes I thought I would try something different Amanda told him. I like it Gunnar told her. Amanda was lost in her own thoughts while they ate pizza Gunnar and Kendra was in nonstop conversation. Don't they know I'm hurting inside Amanda wanted to scream at them. You ok honey Gunnar asked? Yes I'm sorry Amanda said I'm just sitting here enjoying your conversation.

 I love your hair Kendra told her oh and I talked to Mad today and she asked grandma if she could get her hair cut but grandma told her she had to get permission from you.  Well I'm going up Amanda told them tomorrow is Thursday so I'll be off for three days maybe we can go see a movie. Can Kevin come too Kendra asked? Amanda looked at Gunnar to get his expression but he said yes I think he's a nice boy and I like his parents. Did you know they were from Michigan he asked Amanda? No I had no idea. Sunday night Amanda laid in bed with her eyes open the last time she looked at the clock it read three thirty then when she closed her eyes the alarm came on. She felt hot and cold at the same time while in the shower she thought about Anthony.

Anthony was a far cry from the man she had fallen in love with so long ago. When she first started talking to him she was lonely and he made her smile, she was low and he brought her up, she was weak and he made her strong he changed her from a helpless sheep to a fury wolf. She had noticed the change but was always afraid to question him about it. Anthony had a shadow about him, their conversations were different like his mind was always somewhere else and he had not smiled at her the same way. Now Amanda knew why. At twelve noon Amanda was sitting at her station thinking about going up to the eleventh floor to the cafeteria when her cell phone rang. Anthony's name showed up on the caller ID. She pushed the ignore button on her phone then immediately a text came and read come across the street we need to talk I'm sorry.

Amanda left her station with all thoughts running through her head. She didn't realize she was crying until she walked into the restaurant. Anthony kissed her wet tear drops from her face then lowered his mouth on hers. As he French kissed her she felt electricity throughout her body. When he finally pulled away he told her he was sorry and owed her an explanation.

No you don't Amanda told him all the while he was reading the many questions in her face. I wanted to tell you but I didn't know how Anthony started. I wanted to share the entire truth with you the day I found out but I just couldn't find the right words. She knew right then that they had their last lunch together, Amanda saw her friendship with Anthony fading right before her eyes. All the wonderful afternoons they shared fading by the presence of the future to come. She wouldn't feel his lips on hers again, she wouldn't feel his arms around her again, she would miss them smiling at each other over lunch for no reason. All she was left with are the warm memories of Anthony Stevin Moore which she would hold on to forever. She was blinded by the harsh reality that she would never see him again.

For the next month Gunnar noticed Amanda wasn't her usual self. She was like a robot just doing her every day chores and nothing else. The smile was gone off her face, little fine lines appeared on the condor of her eyes and Gunnar contributed it to her missing her parents. One night after dinner he suggested they drive to New York to pick up Madison. We can get a suit for a week and catch some shows.

"No I don't want to". Amanda sighed. Well what about Florida for a week on the beach? Amanda just sat there staring into space. Earth to Amanda come in Gunnar laughed. I'm trying to cheer you up here, I know Amanda said I'm just a little depressed. Do you want to talk about it Gunnar asked? One of my co-workers lost her mom three weeks ago and we all loved her very much. She would send warm muffins to the job, even the sergeants looked forward to her muffins. I'm so sorry Gunnar said, why didn't you go to the funeral? You know how I am about funerals Amanda said, I rather remember you laughing then to have my last memory of you in a casket. Ok I'll order Mad's plane ticket Gunnar said.

The next week Gunnar drove Gunnar Jr. to the airport to catch his plane to Maryland with three suit cases full of new clothes and a pre-paid credit card in his wallet. Gunnar hugged his oldest son goodbye and told him to call when he arrived. During the two hour flight Gunnar Jr. tried to talk the stewardess into giving him an alcoholic drink. When he saw that she wouldn't budge he tried to get her phone number. The stewardess gave him a sweet smile and told him that she was married. Oh no don't want that again Gunnar Jr. clarified. You been married the stewardess asked with a raised eyebrow? Yes, too many secrets he told her. When Gunnar got off the plane he went to retrieve his bags. He took one of the waiting cabs outside to the college. When he finally found his dorm room there were already two freshman's there to greet him. We were wondering where you were one boy said. Yea we thought you had changed your mind about college and realize it wasn't for you the other boy laughed.

Are you kidding me Gunnar answered? Anything to be out on my own. No mom breathing down my back, no little brother wearing my clothes. You won't wear my clothes without permission will you he asked them. I don't know let's see what you got the boy's laughed taking the suit cases from Gunnar laying them on his bed and opening them. Where are you from Gunnar asked? I'm Miguel and I'm from Mexico one boy said. I'm Peter and I'm a rich white kid from Long Island Peter smiled. What about you Peter asked?

Gunnar from Michigan he announced. When he said Michigan the room got quiet, it didn't sound as exciting as Mexico or Long Island, my dad is from Germany Gunnar spoke up fast. Wow are you kidding me Miguel asked excited the smile coming back to their faces? Does he speak German Peter asked? Also excited to know a German. A little Gunnar told them. Maybe you can teach us a few words. Then they heard a loud bell coming from outside, well guys I believe lunch is ready Miguel said. Gunnar loved his college and on the first day he met lots of friends including girls.

The day Madison arrived back in Michigan the house got noisy again. She accursed Kendra of using her hair brush and her strawberry shampoo. Gunnar and Amanda was standing in the kitchen and heard her arguing with her sister upstairs. Well welcome home Madison Gunnar laughed. With only one week left of summer break Gunnar suggested they take a four day cruise. No not this time Amanda said maybe for thanksgiving. Ok you're the boss Gunnar said. Amanda was overdue at the beauty shop and couldn't put it off any longer. She didn't want to face Jalaya thinking she might read her thoughts.

Mom when are you going to the hair dresser Madison asked coming into the kitchen? I saw a cute little shop that opened on Main Street Amanda told her daughter and I was thinking about going there. I don't want to go there Madison pouted. I want to go to the same shop you've been going to for fifteen years. What are you going to have done to your hair Amanda asked? I'm going to have it all cut off in the back and on one side Madison told her. A style I saw in the magazine at grandmas.

Amanda looked at Gunnar to read his expression. It's your hair, do what you want Gunnar told her.

Madison ran to her dad and gave him a big hug, thank you daddy, I love you Madison squealed. When can we go Madison asked? Right now if you want Amanda told her. On the drive to the shop Amanda was hoping Jalaya wasn't there. When she and Madison walked in she was relieved to see another girl at the shampoo station. Must be her day off Amanda thought. Hey girl where you been the owner called from the back. There's a package for you behind my desk. For me Amanda asked surprised? Yes from Jalaya she left two days ago going back to college. Amanda thought to herself I didn't know she was in college she never talked about it. Who's Jalaya Madison asked? She's the girl that shampoos my hair when I come here Amanda told her. Madison went first and while the girl shampooed her hair Amanda retrieved the beautiful warped box from behind the desk. When she opened the box inside was a beautiful picture frame with their picture in it that they took at the mall. Jalaya had gotten the pictures blown up to fit the five by seven frame and on the bottom of the frame it had "Friends Forever."

When Madison was allowed to look in the mirror she let out a loud squall, this is exactly the way I wanted it, thank you so much she said giving the hair dresser a big hug. Amanda and Kendra loved her hair cut. Maybe I'll get mine cut next Amanda said. Gunnar wouldn't let Traci or Kendra fill his kids head with nonsense like Santa Clause he didn't want them thinking a fat white man was bringing them toys when it was his money buying all the expensive toys. Or the tooth fairy who would come into their bedroom at night and take their tooth from under their pillow to make pearls out of it and leave a quarter under their pillow. But it was always him that took the tooth from under their pillow and left the dollar when they fell asleep. Or the Easter bunny that magically left a basket full of chocolate on the kitchen counter for the children to find in the morning.

Gunnar Jr.'s first years as a college freshman went smoothly. He kept his grades up and stayed out of trouble. He had put his parents through enough and it was time for him to grow up. He had three siblings behind him to show an example. Major was passing all his senior classes and looking forward to his graduation next week.

 Amanda called Charlotte to ask her if she wanted to meet for lunch. Sorry cousin but I have a date. With big Mike Amanda asked? Nope with Clarence, who is Clarence Amanda asked, what happened to big Mike? He's still around Charlotte laughed, listen I have to go Clarence will be here in ten minutes and I'm not ready yet. Ok let me speak to Aunt Susan Amanda said. Why don't we try for next week Charlotte asked? No next week is Majors graduation and I don't know what Gunnar have planned.

 Gunnar ordered Gunnar Jr.'s Plane ticket to come home for the summer. Well guys maybe we will get to room again next year Gunnar told Miguel and Peter. Miguel was doing summer school because he couldn't afford to fly home for the summer. Peter's parents sent their private plane to pick him up from school. Gunnar Jr. took a cab to the Maryland Airport and his dad met him at the Airport in Michigan. He gave his dad a big hug and told him all about his first year in college. Well I hope you got some work done amongst all that excitement his dad said. Check this out Gunnar Jr. said handing his dad his grades I passed all my classes. Well this calls for a celebration Gunnar said. Hey dad you think we can stop for a beer? Oh you're drinking now Gunnar asked? No dad just one beer every once in a while. After they stopped for beer Gunnar dropped him off at home. When Gunnar Jr. Walked into his house Major met him at the door. Congratulations brother Gunnar told him, you made it through high school.

Yea, yea whatever. Major tells his brother, "I don't approve of mom seeing this Marcus guy. I think she should date someone her own age". Gunnar Jr. Tells his brother that he needs to mind his own business and leave it alone.

 Dominique was released from the Institution and when Patricia brought her home she felt she had to raise her daughter all over again. She put her life on hold to care for her daughter. She stopped dating, she stopped meeting her girlfriends for lunch she even stopped sleeping in her own room and slept in the other twin bed in her daughter's room at night to keep an eye on her.

 Everything was going great at Majors graduation while Gunnar, Amanda, Kendra, Madison, Gunnar Jr.

and Traci sat and waited for the graduates to march in. That's until they spotted Major marching down the aisle, him and three other seniors had decided to wear their robes inside out. When the three were seated an official went to them and made them put the robes on the correct way. After the graduation they all went to dinner and after dinner Major went to hang with his friends and stayed out the entire night. Traci slept on the couch all night waiting for him to come home. When he did come home at nine in the morning Traci scolded him and Major asked her not to tell his dad. Two weeks later they all went on a cruise and Traci was glad to have the house to herself for one whole week even though she only spent one night there, the rest of her nights were spent at Marcus house.

Jalaya flew home that summer anxious to see her baby brother. Anthony had sent her many pictures but she wanted to hold him and hear him laugh. Anthony Jr. was born weighing seven and a half pounds and nineteen and a half inches long. Anthony was so proud of his son and everyone around him noticed. His brother Big Mike told Anthony he looks just like his son Mike Jr. Jalaya didn't work that summer, she stayed at home playing with her baby brother. Her uncle Big Mike came over and told them he was thinking about asking his girlfriend to marry him. So when do we get to meet her Anthony asked his brother? Soon big Mike told him, what's her name Tiffany asked? Charlotte big Mike answered with a big smile on his face. You look like a man in love Anthony teased, and gave his big brother a hard hit on the shoulder.

 When they returned from their cruse Amanda called Charlotte to tell her what a wonderful time they had. When was the last time you and Gunnar went on a cruise by yourselves Charlotte asked? Or any place romantic without the kids? You knew him before me you know Gunnar don't have a romantic bone in his body Amanda told her cousin. When was the last time you had a romantic dinner together Charlotte asked? "Umm" just what I thought Charlotte said. Wait I'm thinking Amanda said. When was the last time he brought you flowers Charlotte asked? I don't remember Amanda told her in a low voice. He did come to my job last March and we walked hand and hand to a little restaurant down the street and he surprised me that night. With what Charlotte asked? We had the best love session we ever had. It was like he was a different person. I was going to call you but I fell asleep Amanda told her. Wow that must have been some love session if you fell asleep afterwards. And did you dream about it Charlotte asked? Well actually no Amanda said, I dreamed about me and you in high school. I rest my case Charlotte said. What does that mean Amanda asked? Bye Amanda I'll call you back later Charlotte said and hung up.

The next time Jonnie went to Michigan was a year later when Kendra graduated from high school. Frank told her he was not going because once in a life time was about all he could take of seeing Gunnar Bradley.

Amanda took Kendra shopping three weeks before graduation. Spend whatever you need to Gunnar told them. After graduation the family would be going on their cruse then Kendra would be leaving for Yale, only coming home once a year for summer break. Kevin didn't make the grades to get into Yale but the two would communicate by text and through the computer. Gunnar and Amanda was so proud when Kendra's name was called to walk across the stage to get her diploma. Jonnie handed Amanda a tissue and then used one on her own eyes. Kevin sat there with a big smile on his face happy for her.

After the graduation they all went to dinner. Gunnar noticed Kevin and Kendra whispering and smiling at each other and remembered when he use to smile at Amanda the same way. Then Gunnar had an idea. Kevin do you think your parents would let you go on our cruse with us this year? Are you kidding me Kevin asked? No sir they wouldn't mind at all. My treat Gunnar told him. Thank you daddy Kendra said running to the other side of the table to give her dad a hug. I guess you'll be sharing a room with us Gunnar Jr. said yea you can have the top bunk because I have the couch Major laughed. I don't care I'll sleep on the floor Kevin said.

 Well since everyone is in a good mood I have good news Charlotte announced. All eyes went to her and she told them she has two proposals and have to choose one. Well now congratulations are in order Gunnar said and got the waitress attention and ordered a bottle of wine. Who's the lucky guy Gunnar asked, anybody I know? No I don't think so Charlotte said. Big Mike is my boss and Clarence is my neighbor. Is that Clarence Wallace Gunnar asked? You know him Amanda asked? Oh yea I forgot you, me and Clarence went to that party when I first moved back home from New York Charlotte said. He's a nice guy Gunnar said but you'll have to make your own decision we can't help you with that.

 3 years later Gunnar Jr.'s graduation from college was a big deal. He drove to his dads to ask Amanda if she could press the wrinkles out of his gown, he said he didn't trust his mom to do it. Sure Amanda smiled and took the gown from him and headed to the laundry room. She heard the doorbell while she ironed Gunnar Jr.'s robe then she heard voices. When she walked back into the room Charlotte and her fiancé Clarence was standing there and she was showing off the big diamond on her finger. Gunnar, Gunnar Jr. and Clarence went into the den for a drink. I'm so happy for you Amanda told her giving her a hug, and a little Jealous. I'm sorry Charlotte said I didn't mean to hurt you. Its ok Amanda told her cousin.

Gunnar bought every ones ticket to Maryland even Traci's. He was so proud of his son, he gave him a plane ticket to fly anywhere in the world he wanted. After they all returned to Michigan Gunner Jr. was offered a management position at AT&T. After working at AT&T for three months he started to think about Dominique again and wondered how she was. After he left the office he decided to drive by to see if her and her mom still lived in the same place. Patricia Clark answered the door and didn't recognized Gunnar Jr. at first until he asked her about Dom, he was the only one she knew that called her daughter Dom. She's not well Patricia told Gunnar Jr. she has never stopped talking about you. She was admitted to an Institution after you went away to college. They kept her there nine months.

When she came home she cried for three weeks straight and they had to take her back. They kept her for eleven months and when I brought her home she went a full three weeks without getting dressed. She never left the house and didn't comb her hair the entire three weeks. When I finally got her to go out she had no interest in anything and no drive to do anything. I have to make her comb her hair every day, she tells me "what's the use no one's going to see me." Where is she now Gunnar Jr. asked? She said she was going for a walk Patricia told him. There she is now Patricia said nodding her head toward the street.

When Gunnar turned around his heart stopped. Dominique had let herself go down the drain. Her hair was matted, her clothes were wrinkled, she was wearing house shoes and she was walking with her head down. When her mom called her name she looked up and saw Gunnar Jr. standing there taller and more handsome than ever. She ran to him and warped her arms around his neck they both stood there crying.

Patricia left them standing there and went back in the house. Why did you come here? Dominique asked him. I never thought I would see you again. Gunnar held her face between his two hands and tilted her face up to his, your mom told me you haven't been taking care of yourself Dom. Then Dominique started to cry again. No one has called me Dom since you left me. Gunnar held her in his arms while she cried. He let her take all the time she needed before he continued.

Why did you lie about the pregnancy Gunnar asked her? I loved you and didn't want to lose you Dominique cried. You wasn't going to lose me Dom, you were my first love. And you were mine Dominique assured him and started to cry again. Your parents thought I was trash and they thought you were too good for me Dominique told him, and after a while I did too. That's why I thought if I told everyone I was pregnant you wouldn't leave me. Oh Dom I'm so sorry you had to go through everything you went through. I'm sorry I put you and your family through so much she told Gunnar Jr.

Come go for a ride with me Gunnar told her, taking her hand and leading her to his car. Gunnar Jr. opened the car door for her and she sank into the soft leather seats. When Gunnar started driving Dominique saw they were heading down town, the opposite way from the hotel she thought he was taking her to. Where are we going she asked Gunnar? You'll see Gunnar looked at her smiling. When he parked in front of Sassoon's Dominique had to catch her breath. Are we going in there she asked him? Yes Gunnar told her. They charge almost $200.00 just for a perm Dominique was saying but Gunnar was already out the car on his way around to open her door.

I can't go in there looking like this Dominique told him still sitting in the car while Gunnar held the door open for her to get out. Do you trust me Gunnar asked holding his hand out for her to take? When they entered all eyes turned to Dominique. Gunnar left her standing at the door and went to talk to the lady behind the desk. Dominique stood there looking around, everything around her was white. The walls, the floors, the shampoo sinks, the hair dryers, the lace curtains, the big flower pots holding the firm plants, the seats for the customers waiting even the workers were all in white. Dominique couldn't hear what Gunnar was saying to the lady behind the desk but she kept smiling and looking over at her.

Gunnar and the lady walked toward her and Gunnar took a seat in one of the white leather chairs and the lady told Dominique to follow her. Sassoon spent four hours on Dominique's hair, it was so matted they just had to cut it off. When they left Sassoon's Gunnar told her he never saw her hair cut that short before and he loved it. Sassoon's even arched her eyebrows free. Dominique couldn't stop looking at herself in the car mirror, she loved her short hair cut too. Where to next she asked in her preppy voice?

You'll see Gunnar laughed at her. Are you hungry Gunnar asked her? No I'm too excited Dominique told him. Gunnar's phone rang but he ignored the call. His phone rang three more times and he continued to ignore the calls. When he parked in front of Macy's Dominique's eyes got big as saucers. I would have been just as happy if we went to Kmart she told him. In Macy's Dominique tried on three different outfits and couldn't decide on one so Gunnar bought all three. Gunnar checked his phone while Dominique was in the dressing room. He had one call from his dad and three from his mom, he didn't want them to know what he was doing or who he was with.

He left Macy's spending over $400. On three outfits, underwear and two pair of shoes. Now are you hungry Gunnar asked her when they got in the car? Ravished Dominique laughed. Gunnar found his feelings for Dominique rushing back dramatically dispute everything they went through. Gunnar pulled into McDonalds and they walked in hand and hand. Dominique took her fluffy house shoes off in the car and put on her new black sandals. When they walked into McDonalds it was like the last four years had never existed.

Do you still like Big Mac, fries and chocolate shake Gunnar asked? Don't forget the extra pickles Dominique laughed. Oh yea I forgot about the extra pickles Gunnar laughed. They ordered their food and walked to their favorite table. Hey what happened to our names that were engraved on this table Dominique asked? It looks as though they got new tables Gunnar said while expecting the table looking for their names. Gunnar Jr. and Dominique sat there talking after they ate their food and Gunnar's phone rang four more times showing Traci's name on the screen.

You should answer it Dominique told him, it might be important, you don't have to tell them you're with me. Hello Gunnar said answering his phone when Traci called again. Traci never said hello, she was so excited "Marcus asked me to marry him" and I said yes. That's nice mom Gunnar said, I like Marcus. But what about Major, Traci asked, what is he going to say? He thinks Marcus is too old for me. Do you love him mom Gunnar Jr. asked? Yes I do Traci told her son and Gunnar could hear the happiness in her voice. Well do it mom, don't let anyone steal your happiness. Major will be moving out next year when he graduate from MSU and you will be all alone.

As Gunner Jr. hung up the phone he sat and smiled looking into Dom's eyes. He spent a few minutes thinking about his family, his mother and brother. His smile grew even larger as he began to think about how everything seemed to be falling in place in everyone's life. Dom touched Gunner's hand, "are you alright?"

Yeah, Gunner said, "I am just fine and I think everyone else will be too".

The End